Everyone Here Is From Somewhere Else

A Novel

To Mr. Grumpy;

Even you should get a few laughs out of this!

Best,

Jeff Wallach

by

Jeff Wallach

Yep, For Reneé

"A place can never be neutral; wherever you put yourself, the filings are magnetized and begin their alignments . . ."

—Frances Mayes

"All journeys have secret destinations of which the traveler is unaware."

—Martin Buber

"Travel is where you go to discover your true home."

—Phillip Elliot

"May your spirit live, may you spend millions of years, you who love Thebes, sitting with your face to the north, your eyes beholding happiness."

—From the Wishing Cup of Tutankhamun

Prologue
Howard Carter

PHILLIP AND SPENCER ELLIOT were visiting their mother at Willow Gardens for what would prove to be their last time all together. Jenny kept opening the refrigerator. She was looking for her pearls, she said. Her hair was crazy.

"Did you look in the tuna salad? Or maybe suspended in the Jell-O?" Spencer, the younger brother, asked. He was only half joking; it was the kind of thing their mom might have done to some specific purpose when they were growing up—she once surprised Spencer by hiding the key to his first car, a gift from her, in a pile of mashed potatoes.

Jenny tottered into the living room and sat in the recliner opposite her sons. Phillip straightened a few books on a low shelf. Some were upside down, others arranged with the pages, not the spines, facing outward.

"I want you boys to promise me something," Jenny said. She combed her hair with her fingers, looking at them with one eyebrow raised. They knew that expression could belie honest confusion or intentional befuckery. One moment Jenny might share a story about her girlhood in Brooklyn in great detail—a story about perseverance or honoring your parents or that people in general were liars and shitheels. The next she might whisper that Mrs. Globerman next door was a Ukrainian spy.

"You need to move away," Jenny announced. "Both of you. Live in a different place. Even if it's the same place because you can't stand to be separated. Go soon. While you're still young. It'll become part of your legacy."

The brothers smiled at each other. Ruefully. They were no longer young. They were in their fifties, currently unmarried.

"Are you sending us on a quest?" Spencer asked. "Like the old scavenger hunts?"

"Any place in particular?" Phillip asked.

"It doesn't matter *where*," Jenny said. "Things will be revealed to you. Wonderful things."

They considered her words. Their mother was a master of secret keeping, of misdirection. When they were children, her quests and guessing games could lead almost anywhere—but always somewhere unexpected. Or even profound. That was *her* legacy.

"You'll see what I mean when you get there," Jenny said with some finality. "It's what happened to me when I lived in ancient Egypt."

The boys nodded at each other in the sign language that defined brotherhood, particularly theirs.

"Oh, and have some kids for fuck's sake," their mother added.

Part One

Phillip and Spencer

Chapter One

Nanu Nanu

PHILLIP AND MARTY AGREED that she would be in charge of the wedding. Phillip had bullied his imprint on their first wedding, at Tavern on the Green in Manhattan, and, well, they knew how that marriage had worked out.

"We're going to have this one in Iowa," she told him. They were sorting through his closets in the apartment on the Upper West Side to make room for her things. Again. She would hold up one of his older suits that he didn't seem capable of getting rid of, and give him that look. Phillip would nod and toss it onto the Goodwill pile. He wouldn't need a suit in Iowa. They'd probably wear barrels held up by suspenders. Like the characters in the board game Go For Broke that he and Spencer played as kids. Maybe he wouldn't need suits again in New York, either. Suddenly anything seemed possible: maybe he'd trade his khakis and button down Oxfords for board shorts and third-world-dictator shirts. Maybe they'd become nudists.

"Okay, then," Phillip said. "Iowa!" He smiled at Marty with his marriage smile. Then it transposed to a real smile because of the way he loved her after all this time.

"At the fairgrounds," she added, to test him.

"The fairgrounds. Of course," Phillip said.

"I'm half kidding about the fairgrounds," Marty added. "But only half. They have an event space . . ."

The phrase "event space" conjured debacle for Phillip. He pictured children fleeing a disheveled clown.

"We could have your high school cafeteria cater it," Phillip said. "We could have a merry-go-round for the New Yorkers where they ride real ponies and pull down doughnuts instead of brass rings."

"We could have rainbow unicorns," Marty said. "Pooping out

1

communion wafers with vegetable cream cheese shmears on them for the Jews."

They exchanged vows at the county fairgrounds in Devine, Iowa, on a July day when the fields were as green and gold as a Midwestern sports team's logo. The reception was held in a huge modern barn built with solid timbers held together with black metal brackets. Spencer—whose own first wedding had taken place recently—noted that the timbers must have been dragged to the site by ancient Hawkeye slaves since little plant life larger than corn or soybeans was visible for miles.

"And I had no idea corn was actually *grown*," Spencer said as an afterthought. "I thought they made it on a lathe."

Spencer served as best man—just as he had at Phillip and Marty's first wedding, at what Spencer referred to as "Shazbat Shalom," on West 76th Street in 1993.

"Shabbat Shalom," Jenny, their elegantly Bohemian and irreverent mother, had corrected him at the time. She was proud and nervous in equal measure, her family on display. As often happened, she was only half listening to her younger son.

"I like to call it 'Shazbat,'" Spencer said.

"What's 'Shazbat?'" Jenny asked, adjusting her pearls.

"It's what Mork used to say on TV because he couldn't say 'Oh, fuck.'"

Given the bride and groom's age and experience, the current wedding was a less formal affair, not just because of the locale. Phillip still insisted on beer from Oregon, wine from Italy, and Irish whiskey because these had been so well received at his brother's wedding and reflected new connections they'd all made. Local farms provided the food and catering and the band played bluegrass and country western—Marty's choice. It included actual fiddlers.

As Phillip snuck a moment of repose in a peeling Adirondack chair on the lawn behind the barn before the service, Spencer handed him a cigar the size of a chicken leg. What was it about the massive lawns here, anyway, Phillip wondered? Miles of them, immaculately managed within a blade of their lives? He imagined a homeowner sitting atop a riding mower; when he finished it was already time to start again. He envisioned an Escher-like world of continuous mowing.

"It's the Andalucian Bull," Spencer said, indicating the cigar. "For later."

"It's big enough for the whole family," Phillip said.

"Speaking of 'the family.' I just saw Luca Brasi practicing his speech out in the hayfield. He's wearing a straw hat. And overalls. Which isn't surprising—over all," Spencer said.

"Tell him to come in," Phillip said. "Tell him to leave the hay and bring the cannoli."

Spencer smiled his gorgeous, indefensible, rakish smile. "That's just never not funny," he said.

"No. It's never not," Phillip agreed.

———

At the reception Spencer delivered the official toast. He wore a sleek blue suit the color of the dresses of painted chapel virgins, and a white shirt but no tie—a concession to Phillip and Marty calling for a casual affair, so as not to highlight how different the New Yorkers could be. Despite it doing so anyway.

Spencer stood on the click-together parquet of the dance floor with a wireless microphone in one hand and a plastic champagne flute in the other. He was tan and relaxed and radiated the quiet confidence of someone happily married to the right person after a lifetime of miscues. Trisha, his own new wife, was resplendent in a strappy black dress that offset her fiery hair.

Spencer cleared his throat, tapped the mic twice. The echoey room grew quiet except for the scraping of chairs and the distant lowing of a cow, which unsettled several of the out-of-town guests.

"When my brother asked me to be his best man, I was thinking I could just reuse the toast from Phillip and Marty's first wedding," he began, "since it's been so long that you've certainly forgotten it, or maybe you weren't even there. But then I took a closer look at the speech and kept crossing things out—'I hope we'll toast your fiftieth anniversary' . . . nope. 'I hope you'll have a house full of noisy children who play percussion' . . . nope. 'I wish you a goyish mansion in East Hampton with a cadre of homely Russian au pairs . . .' not likely—until all that was left was 'l'chaim.'"

This elicited a few chortles, a few golf claps.

"So I wrote a new toast. With the help of my wife. Who wasn't even born the last time Phillip got married. No, I'm joking about that. I'm nervous up here because I feel like I'm 0-for-1 with the success of my wedding toasts and I really want this one to take. And please somebody give me the signal to shut up if I'm going on too long."

Around the room, half a dozen people moved hands across their throats. Spencer laughed into the mic with a sound like a voicemail sending.

"Oh, a tough crowd. I'll try to make it short." He shot his cuffs the way their mother had taught him to do so many years ago, when he was The Great Spencerini.

"I just want to say that I've loved Marty since Phillip and I both met her at McSorley's Tavern in New York on a spring night back in 1987, and I knew they were meant to be together. I'm not making that up—it's exactly what I said to him at the time. Her laser use of profanities impressed me from the very beginning.

"So maybe Phillip bolloxed it, but now they're back together, and I couldn't be happier. Our mother, Jenny, would feel the same way if she were still alive—she loved Marty, and those two formed a bond that none of the rest of us could ever explain.

"I wish Jenny was here with us now, she loved a good party, too. And this is a good one. We have some celebrity guests making their first appearances in Iowa. Our cousin Leah and her wife, Stephanie. Phillip's childhood friend Max Feingold—that was him playing the wedding march on the bagpipes. My wife Trisha and her parents are here all the way from Ireland: it turns out—get this!—that Trisha's father is, coincidentally, also Phillip's father! But maybe you've already heard about that. It goes along with another fun fact Phillip and I recently learned: that our Uncle Jerry was actually *my* father, but that's a whole 'nother story—which by the way makes cousin Leah my half sister, as well. Don't worry if you're not following, sometimes we can't figure it all out either. We'll draw you a flow chart after the first dance.

"What strikes me standing here today, other than the sound of tractors outside and a genuine fear of tornadoes, is how different our family looks since Phillip and Marty's first wedding; and what better measure of change is there than to consider how things looked when you first married your true love, and then how things look more than twenty-five years later when you marry them again?

"We've been through a lot lately and the very notion of family relationships—even of who we are as brothers and sons and husbands—has taken on new meanings for us. Phillip and I have talked about it, so I can speak for him too. I probably would anyway. We learned that our very essence is defined by our actions—not just by the DNA that formed us—or certainly not the DNA that we *thought* had formed us—and by the choices we make; like whether you ordered the beef or the fish tonight. I hope you went with the beef, since I haven't noticed an ocean around here. Let me just add that our mother, who turned out to be a wizard of misdirection, left a trail for us to follow to all these conclusions."

Spencer didn't mention that while that particular quest set by their mother was completed, another might be in the offing. He looked out over the crowd grouped in circles of eight around tables set with white tablecloths among the hay bales. Guests were grinning, chuckling, guzzling their toast champagne. Phillip and Marty had intentionally intermixed the New Yorkers with the Iowans, mostly just to see what would happen. They seemed to be getting along brilliantly.

"I'm already going on too long here, and Phillip threatened to use the hook on me if I babbled for more than five minutes, so let me close by saying that Phillip and I discovered that we're largely defined by who we choose (especially since we can't choose our family)—and Phillip and Marty chose each other. And then, given other opportunities and intervening years and other romances they chose each other again. What better testament is there to true love?

"So,"—and here he hoisted his flute of champagne—"please raise a glass with me and say 'l'chaim', or 'Sláinte', or whatever they say when someone makes a brilliant and humorous toast in Iowa. And congratulations. And I love you both—Phillip twice as much as the half brother you've turned out to be. And I am now officially shutting up!"

Which, of course, he didn't.

———————

As the reception carried on into the evening and the sun didn't set so much as recede into a flat orange band thinning behind a windbreak of Norway spruce and a grain silo, Phillip made his rounds to chat with Marty's family. To his befuddlement, they mostly drank the Bud

Light that Marty had insisted on adding alongside the citrusy IPA that Phillip had imported from Oregon at great effort and expense.

This was a home game for them, as Spencer had pointed out, and so they were at ease in their Sunday clothes with their taste-free lager despite the upscale couture of some of the New Yorkers.

After the cake from Walls Bakery on Long Island had been cut and plated, Phillip sidled up to Marty and put his arm around his wife while she spoke with her parents and an old high school friend. Phillip had promised to leave his sense of humor in their Airbnb. The newlyweds agreed that the Iowans were unlikely to "get" Phillip or Spencer.

Marty's father, Dale, was a large, well-groomed man who'd spent years in the sun and wind, but all that weather was behind him now. He'd farmed a family spread outside of town when Marty was growing up, and in the ensuing years added to his holdings while unloading the physical work on others. He was a humbly successful gentleman, both envied and admired by his neighbors. He was an Elks leader, which Phillip found amusing, particularly since there were no real elk in the state anymore. Phillip pictured hunters tracking the old man through the woods. Marty's mom, Cindy, was a sweet, attractive churchgoer whom Marty loved unconditionally.

The Fords had always liked Phillip just fine, despite not really understanding him. Dale particularly admired his son-in-law's in-dustriousness. Cindy was simply glad their daughter wasn't a lesbian. The divorce came as a shock to them and after that—particularly now—they didn't know how to feel. They would try, for Marty's sake, to like Phillip again.

"We're happy to see you back in Devine," Dale said, shaking Phil-lip's hand. Dale loved hand shaking, regardless of whose hand. "I didn't expect this." He waved to encompass Phillip and Marty, Cindy, the event space, Spencer standing with some of the other New York crew and watching the band. Dale was expansive, tipsy in a big, red, farmy sort of way.

Marty's closest childhood friend, Jodi, observed the two men—both of whom loved Marty—interacting.

"Are you thinking of taking over the farm when Dale retires?" Jodi asked Marty.

Marty looked at her father, who stood with his arms crossed over his non-iron twill grid check cotton dress shirt with the French cuffs, acting as if he hadn't heard this. Cindy smiled at a non-existent person in the distance. Phillip nearly shot champagne out his nose.

"What makes you think he'll ever retire?" Marty said. She touched her curly hair, which she was growing out again. Touching it was her poker tell.

"It's quite a spread Dale's put together over all these years. And he refuses to sell," Jodi said. "Plus isn't it time you came home? To carry on his legacy?"

Phillip pictured a series of gruesome images: himself in overalls, chasing a piglet through a cornfield; trying to start the tractor on a 20-below morning. Eating a casserole. And why was everyone suddenly referring to "legacy," for fuck's sake? By "everyone," he meant, so far, one person. But it resonated with what Jenny had said—now nearly two years ago—shortly before she died. And not just about legacy, but about living somewhere else and having things revealed.

"We're still deciding where to live," Marty said. She was being polite rather than telling Jodi she'd sooner live with SpongeBob in a pineapple on the ocean floor than return to her hometown.

"That's the thing about Iowa. There's no place else like it on earth," Jodi said, and Marty's parents nodded.

Exactly, Phillip thought.

But he wondered: did Devine, Iowa, have "wonderful things" to reveal? Was his mother prescient in implying this particular possibility before he'd even gotten back together with Marty?

Nah, he told himself.

But the notion of coming home—to somewhere—struck a chord with Phillip since he was trying to figure out where, exactly, he belonged. And what his own legacy might be. And were these things somehow related? Having found his biological father last year—thanks to Jenny's clues—after half a century of believing he and Spencer had a different father that they never knew anyway, Phillip was reconsidering the very notion of who he was and how to define that. He'd already determined that it was a combination of DNA and kismet, but now the issue of place was elbowing its way to be considered. Just how was where you were from—or where you chose to live—related to who you were, and what you left behind? According to his mother's charge, every place could provide a potential answer—like a door tab on a whiskey Advent calendar. What smooth, smoky flavor might lurk behind the Iowa door?

Lying beside each other in their hotel room later that evening, Phillip said, "Would you ever consider coming back here? To Devine? To live?"

"Are you thinking of working the back forty?" Marty asked.

"Is there really a back forty? Is it really a thing?"

"It's a thing," Marty said. "Although it's almost never actually forty of anything. And I don't know what it's supposed to be in back of. It just means a big, empty piece of land that nobody's using."

"It's fun to say," Phillip said. "Jodi sure wants you to come back—is it something you've considered? Do you have a secret desire to make seven layer salad and play Cornhole at the Grange before the locusts arrive for the season?"

Marty knew that through the joking he was being serious in considering what she might want. This was new for Phillip, and she sought to encourage it.

She turned to him in the small bed, her breath like cake from Walls bakery and toothpaste from Tom's of Maine. "I was done with all this a long time ago," she said. "When people ask me where I'm from, I say New York. I have for twenty-five years. Iowa was a great place to grow up but it hasn't been home for a long time."

Phillip realized for the first time that Marty had defined herself as much by *leaving* Iowa as by becoming a New Yorker. Much as he'd defined himself for so long by being fatherless, and now had to start over.

"It's a relief to me," Phillip said. "I was afraid I might need to take up ice fishing."

"As Billy Joel said, 'Home is just another word for you,'" Marty said, kissing him.

"Well, he also said, 'Ooh ooh oooh ooh, Ooh ooh ooh oooh ooh,'" Phillip pointed out.

"I know exactly how he felt," Marty said.

CHAPTER TWO

"On Many Long Journeys Have I Gone."

AT MOST WEDDINGS, THE bachelor party precedes the ceremony and celebration. But this was not most weddings. Spencer figured that if his brother could marry the same woman a second time *he* could host the bachelor party after the reception. And invite their wives.

On the morning following the wedding Spencer took his brother and the girls on a secret pilgrimage. After sleeping in, and then meeting other wedding guests for a pancake breakfast at the Devine firehouse, the two couples climbed into their rented SUV and headed to, well, none of them besides Spencer knew *where* they were going.

Phillip had dreamed of visiting this destination since he was in his twenties—although he didn't know that it was located in Dyersville, Iowa, he didn't know it was nearby, and he hadn't thought about the place in a long time.

They drove east from Devine on a two-lane highway lined by cornfields. The day was hot and gummy and—Spencer remarked— smelled like salt and melted butter. They passed through small towns with two-block Main Streets lined with two-story brick buildings with hardware stores and fabric stores and adorable antique shops on the ground floors. Ghost signs for businesses that had closed decades ago continued fading on the side and back facades. Men in khaki Dockers and women in print dresses emerged from stone churches, squinting into the sunlight.

Phillip kept guessing where they were headed, though he knew his brother wouldn't reveal their destination even if he figured it out. It was like one of their mom's lateral thinking puzzles about the arm in the parcel, or the man who hung himself, or the carrot, the scarf, and the pieces of coal.

9

"We're going to a parade and I'm the Grand Marshall?" Phillip ventured.

Marty flipped through a magazine that was either about fashion or outdoor adventure—it was impossible to tell the two subjects apart these days—beside him on the dual-colored leather back seat. Trisha sat with her bare feet against the glove box up front, her compact, freckled legs at perfect right angles. She thought it great fun riding through the countryside on the wrong side of the road.

When nobody responded Phillip said, "It's a square dance. An antique car show. A sock hop. It's a Frank Lloyd Wright house. It's the world's largest pig. The world's smallest pig. A hot air balloon festival. Oh, wait, it can't possibly be anything other than a corn maze! It's a corn maze."

Continued silence. They passed a road sign for a winery.

"Oh, for fuck's sake it's not a winery?" Phillip asked.

"Good God, no," Spencer said. "I'm assuming the grapes on that billboard are an artist's rendering? I hope they're not actually growing grapes and making wine in Iowa. It would be like vegan brisket. Or a turducken."

"How is it like a turducken?" Phillip asked.

"What's a turducken?" Trisha piped in.

"I'm afraid to tell you," Marty said, placing her hand on the back of Trisha's seat and leaning forward. "It's a turkey. Stuffed with a chicken. That's been stuffed with a duck," Marty said. "And I'm not joking."

"Do you eat it or shoot at it?" Trisha asked.

"Are we going to see a *talking* pig?" Phillip tried.

"Nyet," Spencer said brusquely. "And Mr. Haney is out of town, if that's your next question," he added, running with his brother's reference to a favorite TV show they watched as kids.

Right before they turned off the highway onto a smaller road that cut through the corn, Phillip saw the sign for their destination. His face transformed from expressing the joy of recognition to revealing something deeper.

"Christ on a pitcher's mound," he said, sounding like his brother—something each of them occasionally did. "It's the motherfucking Field of Dreams!" And he began weeping like only a man who'd grown up without a father could weep at a sappy baseball movie that also had the power to reach the deepest, most hidden part of him, and let him see clearly through the metaphor of a father and son playing catch, what he had missed. Spencer teared up too, as a boy who loved movies more than anything and remembered every line from them, and who had a brother who wept every time the handsome old baseball player first showed up on the ball field looking confused.

They motored down the long, dusty driveway toward the diamond. Phillip leaped from the vehicle before it came to a full stop in the parking lot beside the old white house. He ran straight out onto the perfectly mown grass. He sprinted through the outfield and disappeared into the tall corn beyond—just so he could emerge back out of it the way Ray Liotta did in the movie. Standing in the outfield again, he bent over with his hands on his knees and cried.

Other visitors stopped their pick-up game around the infield and looked at the kooky middle-aged man in the fancy clothes. Possibly they thought he had a corn allergy.

When Spencer and Trisha and Marty caught up to him in the grass—Trisha wondering "what the what?"—Phillip was laughing through his tears.

"It's okay, I was just talking to the corn field," he said, stealing a line from the film.

Spencer summarized the movie for Trisha, explaining how the son of a damaged father heard a cornfield talking to him so he built a baseball field so that dead players who cheated in the 1919 World Series could meet James Earl Jones and Burt Lancaster and save a little girl from choking on a hot dog, and then Kevin Costner could play catch with his own father, who was somehow younger than Costner and wore a cool uniform, before they all disappeared back into the corn.

Trisha seemed puzzled. "So, wait: it's a movie about a dead baseball player?"

"It's a movie about a whole *team* of dead baseball players," Spencer said. "And now that I think of it, Kevin Costner's wife in the movie looks a lot like *you*. I mean, a *lot*. Amy Madigan. Look her up! Holy leprechauns, I never realized it before." And then Spencer started to cry.

"She married Ed Harris," he said through his sobs. "Who played Jackson Pollock. People called Ed Harris the thinking woman's sex symbol. Which is different than me—I consider myself the eejit woman's sex symbol. Present company excluded," he added.

When the sobbing had run its course they wandered toward the infield, where a ragtag group of kids and adults were going through the inexplicable motions of baseball.

"You wanna join?" a young boy asked from where he was playing shortstop. "We could use four more to make a real game."

Phillip looked at the others. "Put me in coach," he said.

So they joined, filling empty positions. Marty took up a post at second base, where she hoovered grounders and made several wild throws to first, cursing heartily then putting her hand over her mouth when the kids stared at her. Spencer and Phillip played right and center fields.

"Don't we need a catcher?" Spencer said, quoting *Field of Dreams* again with a line that nobody would possibly remember.

The kid playing third base in a full uniform answered, "Not if you get it near the plate we won't," to Spencer's great delight.

Trisha, who had no idea what to make of any of it, took over behind home—standing well behind the batter with a catcher's mitt she kept examining at as if she'd suddenly discovered she held a handful of flaming kittens.

"Why are you standing back so far?" the pitcher—someone's dad—asked Trisha.

"Because that kid's swinging a *club*," she said.

When it was his turn to bat, Spencer knocked a long ball along the left field line and ran the bases like a greyhound chasing a fake rabbit, his expensive hiking boots—which he'd never worn hiking—kicking up clouds of infield dirt. Phillip lined one over the shortstop for a single. Marty, who was sporting a backward ball cap, knocked a pop fly that was caught behind second base but Spencer tagged up and made it home before the mom who caught the ball got over her surprise and remembered to make the throw.

Trisha, against all odds, went after a pitch in the dirt and executed her perfect golf swing, blooping one into the outfield, but she ran to third base—arms pumping, the tattoo on her exposed upper back flexing—because she'd just seen Spencer come from there, and a confused teenager tagged her out. She nearly took a swat at him, not understanding this was part of the game.

They played four innings before the other folks headed toward the gift shop. The two couples sat in the stands where, Spencer explained to Trisha, one of the ghost ball players who later becomes a doctor played by Burt Lancaster saves Kevin Costner's daughter but has to give up the baseball career he never had before also disappearing into the corn.

Trisha nodded. "This film just keeps getting better," she said.

The brothers sat side by side, looking up occasionally at the delicious crack of an ash Louisville Slugger from where a new group of tourists was taking batting practice.

"That was awesome," Phillip said to Spencer.

"Was it heaven?" Spencer asked.

"It's Iowa," Phillip replied, filling in the blank of the emotional movie Mad Libs that his brother kept setting before him.

Spencer said, "I considered inviting Patrick to come with us—you know, your new actual father. But I thought that might have been a little over the top. Plus he pitched three innings of relief yesterday and I didn't think he was ready yet."

"For me this place has always been about being fatherless, the way we grew up," Phillip said.

"That's what I thought. It's about the *idea* of the father."

"Just right," Phillip said.

"It's what W.P. Kinsella would have wanted," Spencer said.

"Who's W.P. Kinsella?" Marty asked. She was still wearing the baseball glove that she'd found at second base. She was punching it with the other hand, looking ready for another four innings. Marty loved baseball. She'd played on a softball team in Central Park when she and Phillip first met. He loved to watch her throw the ball sidearm—which she'd learned right here in Iowa.

"He wrote *Shoeless Joe*, the novel that they based *Field of Dreams* on. Everybody always forgets the writers in these things."

"Why was Joe shoeless?" Trisha asked. "Did someone boost his shoes? Did he trade them for chewing tobacco?"

"He had blisters from new cleats one time, so he took them off and played in his socks. Someone in the stands called him a 'shoeless so-and-so,' and the name stuck."

"Hey, Marty," Trisha said. "Let's go see if we can find some chewing tobacco in the gift shop. I'm starving." She moved her jaw like she was chewing a fat wad of Copenhagen. They walked together toward the shed where you could buy a wooden bat mug or a *Field of Dreams* dog collar, or a replica of the Volkswagen van that Kevin Costner drove while kidnapping James Earl Jones from Boston to Iowa.

"I am so glad we came here. This was a beautiful gift," Phillip told his brother when they were alone. "But just so you know; I'm done with fathers for a while. And probably baseball, too." He picked a splinter from the pine bleacher. "How about you?"

Spencer leaned back with his elbows on the bleacher row behind him. He surveyed the field, the corn. He looked into the Iowa distance as if expecting to see a line of car headlights winding back toward . . . where? Cedar Rapids? Dubuque? He tried to think of the names of other places in Iowa.

"I'm done, too." Spencer said. "In the movie Ray Kinsella says that he never forgave his father for getting old. We had the opposite problem. We never got to see him get old. We never got to see him at all. At least the father we thought was our father. But we've solved that particular mystery." He sat forward again, elbows on knees. "Because you realized that Mom's clue *was* a clue. Even through her Alzheimer's. And she only gave that clue to you."

"Yeah, what about Mom?" Phillip asked. "What about the other quest, that she gave to both of us? I've been thinking about what she said that last time we saw her together at Willow Gardens. About living somewhere else."

"I've thought about it too. It makes me angry," Spencer said. "She's still manipulating us from beyond the grave. It's creepy. And dysfunctional. She was like a dysfunctional Yoda with her insights. Demented, she was. Who was she to talk about our legacies, anyway? What did *she* leave behind—I mean other than *us*?"

"And yet . . . is something waiting to be revealed?" Phillip asked. "I've been thinking of going to Portland for a while. To get a general feel for whether something else is going to show itself. You remember General Feel. He was one of the characters in Clue."

"That was Colonel Mustard. It was usually him with the candlestick in the conservatory," Spencer said. "It took me a long time to figure out how you'd kill someone with a candlestick. At first I thought it meant that they were set on fire.

"At any rate, Trisha and I are considering living in Ireland for a while so she can be near her family. So I'm sort of fulfilling what

Mom challenged us to do, too. But grudgingly. I almost don't want to go *because* she told us to do something like this. Like I don't *want* to discover whatever great secret might be waiting for me. Does that make sense?"

"Like most things you say, it makes very little sense."

Spencer flipped Phillip a baseball he'd taken from the field. "Then we're on the same page," he said. "And by the way. Who loves you, brother?"

Phillip seemed to think about this for a while. He wiped at the infield dust that had stuck to his face where his tears had fallen.

"You do?" Phillip asked. "And by the way: this was the best twelfth birthday party ever!"

Chapter Three

Jim Moore's Place

After the wedding, Phillip and Marty flew from Cedar Rapids into Lewiston, Idaho, via Salt Lake City and Minneapolis. They were headed for a week-long honeymoon wilderness trip on the Salmon River—also known as The River of No Return.

Below them, the high desert plains were golden and the green ribbon of the Snake River—which the Salmon flowed into—curled in wide, sweeping curves. In the distance they could see mountains, where the river came from, Phillip knew. He wondered for the first time about the sources of the Hudson or the East River: they must start somewhere, as something different than the flat, copper waterways filled with mob corpses that they became in Manhattan. But it was unimaginable.

After arriving in Lewiston and spending the night at a chain motel, Phillip and Marty bounced for ten hours in a school bus with their fellow river passengers along roads that turned from pavement to gravel to packed dirt on the final part—the part where, Phillip assumed, their young guides would murder them with dull blades and feed their remains to wolverines, if they even had wolverines in Idaho. And were they like wolves, he wondered? Why else would their names start the same way? Were they little wolves? Did that make them 'lupine?' And wasn't that a flower? Phillip recognized, as his brother often quoted from *The Big Lebowski*, that he was "out of his element."

From the put-in at a place called Corn Creek—a synchronicity, Phillip thought, since they'd just been to Iowa—they began their trip riding in one of the beautiful handcrafted wooden dory boats with a middle-aged hippy named Beano plying the oars. His gray ponytail poked out beneath the wide brim of his straw cowboy hat. Beano exuded the quiet confidence of someone who performed a physical job well. He was an artist of the highest caliber, maneuvering them through the riffles and rapids with quick wrist flips.

"Where's home for you, Beano?" Phillip asked, mainly because he was unaccustomed to the vast quiet of the river—something it would take a few days to become comfortable with.

"The Escalante Canyon," Beano said, watching the current rolling out in front of them.

"Where's that?" Phillip asked.

"Um, it's the name of the boat we're in," Marty offered.

"You live in the boat?" Phillip asked.

"You didn't ask me where I live," Beano said. "You asked me where home was. This is home for me. On a river. In a dory. Rowing folks like you."

"Ah," Phillip said, catching on to something he would remember as he sought his own new notion of home.

Beano was open and approachable despite having had this same conversation over and over, week after week, on the same river trip for decades. He knew that each guest was different, and Phillip seemed curious if uninformed. Beano's real job wasn't rowing rich folks down rivers—it was raising consciousness, and maybe some funds, if all went well, to protect places like the Salmon.

"All the dories are named after natural disasters caused by man," Beano said. "Pristine places ruined by development, greed, and overuse. The boats are tributes to those places." He was trying to step outside himself—sometimes he was so focused on rowing and reading the currents and watching for eagles overhead that he forgot there were people riding in his boat.

"So Escalante Canyon is a real place?" Marty asked.

"It's in Utah. Formerly a most astonishing wilderness. Until some jackass wrote a story about it for the cover of *Sierra Magazine* and attracted hordes of backpackers. Many of them weren't equipped for that kind of trip. Others didn't appreciate the wild nature of the place. They played loud music at night and left cigarette butts in the red dirt. Nobody will ever be alone there again with just the otters and the canyon wrens. That disturbs me."

"We don't know much about wilderness, or the west, or country music, for that matter—not that country music has anything to do with the west," Phillip said. "I'm sorry if we sound dumb to you."

"Not dumb," Beano said. "You're just from somewhere else. We all are."

To break the ensuing silence Phillip said, "What's the dumbest question a passenger ever asked you?" He asked partly because he didn't want to *be* that passenger. And he was intrigued by this skinny, mythological figure they'd entrusted their lives to. Phillip wanted to win him over, although he didn't know why.

Beano took a long time answering, as if the choices were vast. "A woman once asked me if when the trip was over we'd end up in the same place as where we started."

"Wow, that *is* dumb" Phillip said, shaking his head. "So do we?"

Beano's face closed in on itself. It took him a moment to recognize Phillip was joking.

"Actually, yes," the guide said. "We chose this river because it runs in a circle. It's very convenient, logistically."

The two men hit it off, which Marty thought as unlikely as a bear and a porcupine becoming friends. In this case her husband was the porcupine.

"Hey, why do they call you Beano?" Marty asked.

"You'll find out on fajitas night," he said.

After a few hours floating the river and eating lunch on a sandy beach beneath massive pines, Phillip confessed to Marty that after all these years in New York maybe—despite what Spencer would say—this *was* his element: the river canyon curving between steep piney hills, the river itself a panoply of sounds and colors and scents, continually changing. Each bend revealing something new: a burbling creek pouring over rounded stones and joining the flow; an abandoned settler's cabin; a moose, for fuck's sake; a natural hot spring carved out of granite.

They both recognized that the backcountry was having an effect on Phillip, but also that he *wanted* it to have an effect. That he was looking for something to happen—"something wonderful," he thought, misquoting his mother. But just because he was trying to find it didn't mean that this wasn't real.

Marty pressed the palm of her hand to his forehead. "Are you alright?"

"I don't know," Phillip said. He giggled like a preschooler. "I think this pristine air is effecting me weirdly. I know what my brother would say . . ."

Marty gave him the "go on" look.

Phillip executed a spot-on impression of what Spencer had said when Phillip told him about the river trip: "Jews aren't supposed to camp. We spent forty years trying to get *out* of the wilderness. You're going to set us back centuries. What river are you thinking of drowning on, anyway?"

Marty laughed. "You've got that down," she said.

"I feel like I've gone back in time," Phillip said, in his own voice, serious again. "Like when we finish the trip we're going to be picked up by a stagecoach driven by a guy with cowboy clothes and half a set of teeth. I fucking *love* it here. And I hate everything."

"Not everything," Marty said. "Just everything new."

At dinner on the second night Phillip enjoyed more than his share of cabernet with the steak and quaffed some whiskey with a warm chocolate cake fresh out of a cast-iron Dutch oven. Marty knew his limited capacity for socializing with strangers, yet he stayed talking to others around the fire when she headed for their tent. When she woke in the cool night and saw that he wasn't beside her, she climbed out with her headlamp. She found him wrapped in his sleeping bag stretched out on the deck of The Escalante, beneath the stars, snoring in time with the gentle rocking of the boat.

The next day he played with other people's children—though he found children thoroughly uninteresting. They were throwing a football in such a way that the receiver had to launch himself into the river to make the catch. Phillip laughed like a madman as he frolicked in the cool green water.

When he came over to her, breathless, and sat beside her on the sandy beach, she whispered, "I've seen *Invasion of the Body Snatchers*. I know what's going on here."

He grabbed her up in his arms and ran with her down the slope to the river, where they tumbled in. She came up trying to be mad, but the sheer joy on her new—and former—husband's face was so overwhelming that she got choked up before dunking him back under the surface.

"This is not normal behavior," she said when he popped up again.

And it continued—fits of childlike mirth alternating with deep, reflective appreciation. *What? The? Fuck?* Marty couldn't stop thinking. Was this a result of Phillip having discovered his father after half a century of thinking he didn't have one? Did it have to do with his recent remarriage to her, she hoped? Was it something to do with this place? Was his mother to thank for it?

Each day Phillip grew more animated about the day's rapids, about cocktail hour before dinner and the whiskey that would follow dessert and the guitar playing around a fire, and even just peeing outside.

One morning he and Marty paddled together in what the guides referred to as "the divorce boat"—a two-person inflatable kayak that proved to be the inspiration of many public marital kerfuffles on commercial river trips. Typically each paddling member of a couple was likely to blame the other for the boat going sideways, or hitting a rock they were supposed to miss, or flipping in a lateral wave. But Phillip parked himself up front and let Marty do the steering. When they did flip he came up dripping wet and grinning.

On the last evening, while their guides gossiped and drank cocktails and prepared the group's final five-course dinner, and some other guests tossed horseshoes and some swam in a big, deep eddy off shore, Phillip leaned back in his camp chair and smoked the Andalucian Bull that Spencer had given him before the wedding. He'd read somewhere that when Native Americans smoked tobacco they blew each puff of smoke skyward as a prayer. He figured this was as good a place as any to do the same—but what to pray for? He figured he'd start with: more days like this.

Marty, watching him, wondered—and worried about—how long Phillip's newfound lightness might last.

The next morning, their final river day, Marty rode in the dory with Beano while Phillip maneuvered the single-person inflatable kayak down their final miles to the take-out at Vinegar Bar. He was reflective, and kept himself separate from anyone else.

"I've never seen him like this," Marty told Beano.

"It happens more often than you'd think," Beano said.

"What does?"

"I don't want to sound like some old stoner,"—though in fact he *was* an old stoner—"but the river changes people. Not just in small ways. Not just for a few days. Wait it out. Something might be at work here."

"I wish I believed you," Marty said. "I've known him a long time. He's not really the changing type. He orders the same two slices every time we go for pizza. He eats them in the same order. He has one fried egg on toast and half a banana for breakfast every single day. He won't get rid of concert tee shirts that haven't fit him since high school."

"You may be right," Beano said. "But . . . nevertheless." He pushed at the oars to avoid a rock in the current. "I mean . . . it is called the River of No Return. And that can be a good thing."

"That's actually why we took this trip rather than the other one," Marty said.

"Which other one?"

"The River of Fucking Tears," Marty said.

Chapter Four

i sing of olaf glad and big

It wasn't as if Phillip had *never* slept outside before the river trip. And it wasn't the first time in his life that he would be redefined by a place—something he and Spencer learned from their mom as she returned from travel agent familiarization trips, always changed. In small ways, like when she added couscous to their dinner rota; and in larger ways, such as when they joined Save the Children after her excursion to India, and when they all donated some of their spending money to help pay for a kid in Rwanda to go to high school.

Each summer, when Phillip and Spencer were kids, Jenny sent them to spend eight weeks at Camp Redwood in the Catskill Mountains—as much for Jenny's sake as their own. It gave their mom a reprieve during which she could behave as an adult for a couple of months, have dinner with a gentleman, and not worry about tripping over a skateboard or a baseball mitt on her way to the bathroom in the night. She also knew the kind of impact a change in place could have on people.

During each of those summers the boys enjoyed one night sleeping in tents that had been set up for them a mile from camp, amidst the thick hardwoods. If they listened while their counselors cooked "hobo eggs" for breakfast the next morning they could hear whistles blowing on the basketball courts back at camp. And yet the campsite, called Tarzan's Lair, seemed of another time and place—possibly from when Tyrannosaurs roamed the hills and ate whatever creatures were hanging around the arts and crafts shack.

Those hot, dripping upstate summers gave the boys an opportunity to remake themselves, to shrug off the personalities and reputations they'd created at school and recreate who they wanted to be. Their mom understood this. Spencer was seven and Phillip nine when

Jenny first sent them to Redwood; Spencer always joked that she'd intended to ship them to Camp Goldstein but it was already filled with Native American kids.

Despite its name, Redwood was a sports camp, and Spencer thrived there. It was his first chance to excel as an athlete rather than being identified as the agent provocateur he'd defined himself as at home—despite an incident when the owner of the camp locked Spencer in the basement of his house after catching him on a midnight raid to a girls' bunk. He'd asked Spencer to promise that he wouldn't come out again after curfew, and Spencer said, "I don't want to make a promise that I'm already planning on breaking." Hence the basement imprisonment.

The brothers talked about the impact of camp often in later years. They'd be together in one of their apartments, or in a bar or restaurant, and a song would come on—say, "Long Train Runnin'," by The Doobie Brothers.

"Wayback Playback," Spencer might say. "Camp Redwood, 1976. This was on the radio when Bonny Silverstein tongue-kissed me behind the social hall. I didn't know what she was up to. I thought she was trying to steal my gum."

"I got my first handjob behind the social hall," Phillip recalled.

"Yeah, but that was from one of your bunkmates," Spencer said.

Spencer grew serious talking about camp. "That's where I first recognized I was a genius with balls of every shape and size. It's funny how a single geometric shape could help define my dazzling personality. I could chase one like nobody's business. Hit it, shoot it, kick it, whatever was required.

"Before then I was the troublemaker. The kid who always had a snappy answer. Then suddenly one summer I was popular because I could shoot lights out on the basketball court or hit to the opposite field in softball. My bunkmates loved me. Girls loved me. Chief Redwood himself would have made me an honorary brave in the tribe."

"It's funny you say that," Phillip said. "I think of myself as defined by the Apache Relay in Color War in 1977. That was the year you pushed the Ping Pong ball with your nose from the flag pole to the front steps of bunk C in record speed and later made three layups and three foul shots without a miss."

That summer Phillip didn't so much redefine as accept himself, settling comfortably into who he already knew himself to be; he discovered that the other kids—and especially the counselors—respected intelligence, too. While he could play a respectable second base and defend in soccer with his lanky speed, he was no match for his younger brother's athletic talents and would always be second to him in physical games. As a camper Phillip's most recognized skill was an ability to catch fish in the murky lake with dense balls of white bread from the dining hall. His secret was filling the balls with jelly. Who knew that fish loved jelly?

At the end of August each summer, counselors and administrators split the camp into two teams for a five-day series of competitions called "Color War." The gold and blue teams faced off in events like volleyball and softball, track, a "Sing Out" in which the teams wrote their own fight songs, and the "Apache" relay, which Spencer always pointed out made no sense since the name of the camp was Redwood, after a tree that grew nowhere near any place the Apaches had ever even ridden through even after getting lost following a wrong turn in Mexico.

The relay involved approximately 150 campers and counselors on each team performing such tasks as the Ping-Pong ball blow, eating a peanut butter sandwich and then whistling the star spangled banner, and other pseudo-athletic endeavors. Phillip was chosen as the Atlas Blue teammate to solve the word puzzles in the relay that year.

He and his opponent, a pimpled spaz from Queens who spent most of camp at the rocketry and ham radio shacks, waited on the porch of Bunk H, shaded by an enormous balsam fir that perfumed the warm August air like strawberries, but still gave a slight whiff of encroaching autumn.

Phillip saw a kid from the opposing team, the Golden Pythons, coming toward them across the lawn from the girls' tennis courts balancing a raw egg on a spoon and running in exaggerated slow motion so as not to drop and break the egg. Phillip's own teammate with the egg and spoon was nowhere in sight even when the opponent arrived and handed over the relay baton, and his nerdy nemesis began work on the word puzzle clues.

Phillip paced the tiny porch. "C'mon c'mon c'mon," he whispered as Rocket Boy scribbled with his pencil, answering several clues almost instantaneously.

But as Phillip glimpsed his own teammate first scampering toward them with the spooned egg way off in the distance, his opponent's pencil paused in midair and remained there, frozen. As the egg runner came close enough for Phillip to see the pizza stains from that day's lunch on his camp tee shirt, Rocket Boy's pencil still hovered. Phillip watched as Rocket Boy put the eraser between his teeth and began biting down on it, gently at first, and then surprising himself when his teeth dismembered it and he nearly swallowed the nub.

Phillip grabbed the baton from Atlas Blue's egg runner and picked up the sheet of clues. He touched his tongue to the eraser of his own pencil then scribbled:

e.e. cummings
Marlon Brando
Tartan

His opponent glared at Phillip over the top of his glasses. Phillip guessed Rocket Boy was stuck on one last clue.

Phillip sped through three more, reading them simultaneously then answering them all at once:

JD Salinger
Emu
First Amendment

A small crowd had gathered around the porch like acolytes waiting for the smoke announcing a new pope. The entirety of Color War might hinge on Phillip beating his opponent to the solution with the maximum amount of time left before the baton would be allowed to pass. The teams would be assessed a ninety-second penalty for each unanswered question.

The final clue was: *Blimp-y Sandwich*. There was always a clue that played on words, or was supposed to be funny, or required some otherwise counterintuitive thinking.

Having been taught by his mother to be an immaculate speller—not to mention a wizard at games and puzzles—Phillip wondered at the spelling of "Blimp-y." He knew the sandwich shop of the same name was spelled "Blimpie." Which suggested that either the crafter of this clue had been careless, which was entirely possible, or crafty enough to intend this spelling to send a different message. Phillip processed this cascade of thoughts. He determined to give the creator of the clue the benefit of the doubt despite his skepticism that others cared about language nearly as much as his mother did.

Which meant that the clue didn't refer to the sandwich chain. At the same time, for no logical reason (except maybe that they rhymed), he associated the name Blimpie with the character Wimpy from the Popeye cartoons—the sloppy, portly gent who was always offering to repay someone on Tuesday for a hamburger he could eat today; though this was unrelated, the vagaries and synchronicity of language provided an extra insight.

Which inadvertently suggested the answer that would make Phillip an Atlas Blue hero for the remainder of Color War and lend him an air of legend for his remaining years at camp—even when people didn't remember why he was a legend—and pave the way for Phillip to lead a life based on the acceptance of intellect as in all regards equal to physical prowess. But also convince him there were few conundrums he couldn't solve by applying himself tenaciously—a trait that carried through his years in good ways and some not so good.

Phillip knew the Hindenburg was a famous blimp that had exploded somewhere over New Jersey. It was the only blimp he could think of.

The hamburger was not just Wimpy's favorite sandwich but also his own, and the marriage of the two words was an ecstasy. He scribbled "Hindenburger!" on his paper—including the exclamation mark—and handed it to the judge, who appeared dazzled long enough that Phillip had to grab the race baton out of his hand and push it into the grubby fingers of his next teammate, who would jump rope, in pajamas, across the soccer field and hand off to someone who would remove the wrenched ankle in the board game Operation, before handing the baton so someone who hit the archery target three times before passing to a teammate who would deliver three tennis balls into the service box, and so on until Atlas Blue won the 1977 Camp Redwood Apache Relay, which ultimately led them to victory in that year's Color War, and provided Phillip with the foundational belief that smart people could also be heroes. Which, he thought to himself with great amusement, was his other favorite kind of sandwich.

Chapter Five

John Merrick

As Phillip lost himself in the notion of a new place—first the Salmon River and then more generally the west—Spencer was in the throes of something, too: he missed Ireland, though he'd only lived there with Trisha for a short while. Returning was his best shot at fulfilling Jenny's last request in spite of his bitterness and skepticism about the whole "wonderful things" discovery she'd promised.

Back in New York after Phillip and Marty's wedding Spencer led Trisha around Manhattan like a tour guide, visiting The Met, the 911 memorial, walking from the Battery to the Upper West Side, passing their evenings at music venues and comedy clubs, and enjoying dinners from Peruvian to Basque to a place in Soho that served one hundred varieties of peanut butter and jelly sandwiches, some pan fried, some grilled.

Up in Spencer's loft one evening, with a percussive rain beating on the cars parked along the street below, Spencer said, "We should talk about the elephant in the room."

Trisha looked around her, as if maybe there was an actual elephant. It wasn't beyond Spencer to have conjured one. He was a magician once, after all, she'd heard. From him.

"So I'm the elephant then?" she asked. There was really never any knowing what Spencer might be talking about, jokingly or in seriousness. Was this a reference to some American T.V. show?

"Where we're going to live," Spencer said.

"Ah," Trisha said. So this was possibly going to be serious. "I thought we agreed to be, em, what did you call it: poly-geographical?"

"Yes. To go back and forth without ever making a commitment. To be nomads, but with better hair than Francis McDormand had in the movie."

"I'm just not prepared to pack up and move to Manhattan," Trisha said. "Not at this point."

"That's not what I'm asking. I'm thinking of staging my own *Escape from New York*. Except without the eye patch."

"That's an obscure movie reference that only you and your brother would recognize?" she guessed.

"John Carpenter, 1981. It's like a mash up between *Blade Runner*, *Godfather Part I* and *The Jetsons*, where Jamie Lee Curtis narrates a death match between Kurt Russell (who's been injected with a timed explosive) and gangster Isaac Hayes. Russell tries to save President Donald Pleasance while Harry Dean Stanton drills for oil in Grand Central Station and Ernest Borgnine is killed in a taxi crash with a briefcase containing the secret to nuclear fusion. There's also a character called 'Girl in Chock Full O' Nuts.' Lee Van Cleef appears for the second time playing opposite someone wearing an eye patch. They decapitate the Statue of Liberty, even though that's stolen from *Planet of the Apes*. The best part is that they're all trying to get to *Queens*."

Trisha nodded, feeling her way through this. She wanted Spencer in Ireland. She wanted it nearly as much as she wanted Spencer. If they resided full-time in Ireland she could keep her gig at Irish tourism. And not have to break up the band, which needed her. And be near her aging parents.

"But the whole 'New York is in my blood' diatribe?" Trisha inquired, referring to an earlier filibuster that Spencer had delivered about his hometown. "The what was it, Boo Hoo in your veins?"

"Yoo Hoo," Spencer corrected. "And the New York thing hasn't really been working for me lately. And I'm trying to make my new wife happy."

"Ah yeah, Yoo Hoo. Yogi Bear drank it," Trisha said

"Yogi Berra," Spencer said, laughing, not certain whether she was having him on. "He played for the Yankees."

"It's always back to baseball with you boys, isn't it? Like some Irishmen feel about hurling." She said it like "her-lin."

"What, like throwing up? Yawning in Technicolor? Downloading dinner? Leggoing your Eggo? Sending your entrée back?" He could go on like this for a while.

"No, her-lin: the sport."

"Oh." He pointed his finger in the air. "You mean where they throw the telephone polls?"

"That's the caber toss," Trisha said. "Hurling is the one where they beat the shit out of each other with curved sticks."

"'If you know your country's history as well as you claim to know it, Mr. Bailey,'" Spencer said in his movie voice—which sounded just like him, only deranged—"'you'd know that the Mayo hurlers haven't been beaten west of the Shannon for the last twenty-two years.'"

They smiled at each other.

"Your accent's still shite," Trisha said. "You sound more like a pirate than an Irish person." She waited.

"That's from *The Quiet Man*. 1952 I think it was. John Wayne goes to Ireland and falls in love with Maureen O'Hara while getting outbid to purchase the farm he was born on and they trick someone into almost marrying an old widow and there's some kerfuffle having to do with furniture and a dowry and some boxing and assorted fistfights and the whole thing ends with a weird look of surprise on someone's face."

"I don't know how to compete with that," Trisha said. "There's nothing I can say. But back to the elephant. You'd consider living back home, in Ballydraiocht? Like, in a house, together? Every day? What'll you do?"

"Well, I'd fly back to New York in the evenings, but yes. You and me in the little cottage by the sea. I'll teach you how to make a cup of coffee that's less murderous. I'll practice my short game on the bonnie links."

"You could play in the band. You could make kreplach for dinner. Did I say that right?

"Dinner?"

"I'm going to kreplach you in a minute, mister, if you're not careful."

"It would be my inexplicable pleasure," Spencer said.

She loved him, and not just because he was the only person she'd ever heard say the word 'inexplicable' out loud. She loved him because he wouldn't ask her to move to New York, and for various other reasons.

"We'll see how you feel about this tomorrow," Trisha said, but with hope that they were headed back to Ireland sooner—and for longer—than she'd anticipated. Home, at least for her, since he wasn't sure where his was anymore.

"Let's stay in New York through Thanksgiving," he said, revealing that he'd already thought it through some. "And go back for Christmas so we don't have to eat Chinese food with all the other Jews."

CHAPTER SIX
John Bartholomew Tucker

AFTER SURVIVING WHIPLASH AND Elkhorn and other rapids on the Salmon River, as well as dinner in a restaurant in Lewiston, Phillip and Marty headed for Portland. The Rose City, also known as "Stumptown," had left a mark on Phillip during his brief time there while on the lam from dealing with the notion of his new father. Might a few weeks—or more—reveal what it was that had captivated him? And also unveil the kinds of wonderful things that a person might discover by moving somewhere new?

They rented an Airbnb in the Hawthorne neighborhood—located in a building called The Asylum because the block had originally been home to the local hospital for the insane. They ate dinner the first weekend at a pod of food carts with outdoor tables and fire pits and twinkling lights strung like blinking constellations. Phillip chose a spicy pad thai and Marty ordered a sushi burrito; a barbecue cart in the pod perfumed the neighborhood with the scent of grilling meat. Afterward they wandered the leafy streets of Craftsman and Victorian houses. Lights were coming on inside the houses, revealing glimpses of original dark trim and pocket doors, leaded glass windows, and built-in bookcases. Adorable cats considered the couple from covered porches. People passing on the streets nodded and smiled.

Just before dusk they found themselves at the gates to the Lone Fir Pioneer Cemetery. Phillip had loved graveyards since he was a boy. He took Marty's hand as they ambled among the headstones.

"I could stay here," Phillip admitted to his new and former wife.

"In this cemetery? It would get cold at night."

"There's something about this city," Phillip said. "It's like what cities were supposed to be like before they became, well, cities. It's like a grimy New York windshield has been removed and I can see

31

clearly for the first time. I've noticed that trees are *green*! I feel like if we lived here I would run into people I knew driving on the highway."

"You don't know anyone here. And there's no baseball team," Marty said, playing devil's advocate.

"The Portland Pickles!" Phillip said. "Not the most ferocious of mascots, but still."

"You seem at least half serious about this."

"I'd say between thirty-five and fifty percent. Could you see us staying for a while? Trying Portland on like a shirt?"

"I think it would depend on the type of shirt," Marty said. "For one thing, it would have to be unisex. It would have to fit us both."

"Not a puffy shirt."

Marty caught the Seinfeld reference. "No, not a puffy shirt."

"It would have to be plaid. Red and black plaid."

"A lumberjack shirt. But cut narrow. You could wear it to work in the woods, cutting down trees, and I could wear it to sleep on cold nights, before I load your lunchbox with sushi burritos."

"I'm going to make some calls tomorrow," Phillip said.

"Why not? I didn't take three months off from work for nothing. Let's fuck some shit up," Marty said, surprising even herself.

Those calls started with one of the three young real estate professionals Phillip had met on his previous visit. He hadn't bought the apartment building they had for sale then, but following lunch and too much sake, he'd felt connected to them. As if they were who he might have become if he'd ended up in Oregon.

One of the men offered to meet him for drinks a few days later. Drinks became dinner. Trevor invited his wife and Phillip phoned Marty, who was full of exhilaration following a long run in Forest Park.

"I'm high on chlorophyll," she reported. "I've had too much oxygen. I'm floating near the ceiling."

"Well, get dressed before the buzz wears off and meet us at St. Cousteau's on SE Division. Take an Uber. I think the restaurant is French, but seafood. So maybe snails or oysters or salmon tartare? But it could mean almost anything here."

That night the conversation ranged as widely as Phillip's emotions. The couples hit it off. Trevor told Phillip about a property he was considering buying. Phillip offered to look at it with an eye toward a partnership.

Phillip and Marty drove through the Columbia River Gorge, listening to *Undaunted Courage*, about the Lewis and Clark Expedition.

"How could nobody have told us about this?" Phillip asked.

"About what?"

"That 200 years ago white men hadn't even been here even though they were already ruining Boston and Philadelphia and New York. The stuff about the fur traders and the beaver hats. I knew the history, but they never talk about how frigging gorgeous and green and lush it all is. It's like a south sea island, only colder."

"And rainier."

"That's the name of the mountain outside of Seattle. I never thought about that. I like the rain. I've always liked the rain, except in New York where it liquefies the dog poo and homeless people drape their sleeping bags on the parking signs to dry them out and so you never know where the tow-away zones are."

Phillip pulled their smart car into the tiniest spot imaginable at Multnomah Falls and they climbed to the top in their jeans and hoodies. They were dripping sweat by the time they reached a platform that extended out over the plunging water, offering wide views of the Columbia River.

"We're going to need different clothes for this kind of stuff," Phillip said.

Later, when they'd made their way back down and stopped for a coffee in the stone lodge, Marty said, "What am I going to do out here if we stay?" Marty had arranged a three-month "marriage leave sabbatical" from the PR company where she was a Senior Vice President—something she sorely needed after grinding at the agency for decades.

"Anything you want. Retire. Raise pygmy goats. Raise actual pygmies. Start a foundation. Meditate all day. Read books. *Write* books."

"I think I want to paint," Marty said. "I was thinking that I couldn't possibly give up my job—it's so much of how I define myself. But then I thought: fuck it."

"Yes. Exactly. Fuck it," Phillip agreed.

Two days later Spencer called from New York to see whether Phillip and Marty would be back by Thanksgiving. He and Trisha had news.

"Good God, you're not having a baby at your advanced age?" Phillip asked. "You'd be a grandfather immediately, skipping fatherhood altogether."

"We've decided to adopt . . ." Spencer said. "We're going to start by adopting a highway, and see how that goes."

"We'd love to have Thanksgiving with you, if that's what you're asking. We'll come back for that even if we're not coming back," Phillip said.

"What does that even mean?"

"I bought a building today," Phillip admitted.

"A tree house? A yurt full of shamans? A seedy hotel on Baltic Avenue?"

"An apartment building. Eight units. Built in 1904. I'm going to renovate it."

"You don't even know how to turn on a faucet."

"But I've always been good at finding people who know how to do the things," Phillip said, and that was no lie. While Phillip had spent a career in real estate, his skills didn't reach much below the level of spreadsheets and cap rates and net operating income. He'd recognized his own shortcomings early on—those being nearly anything hands-on practical—and knew his time would be better spent making more money so he could pay plumbers and electricians.

"You have, at that," Spencer admitted. "What did you pay for the building, by the way?"

"I'm embarrassed to tell you. It was under $2 million. I couldn't buy a hot dog cart on the Upper West Side for that."

"Well, hot dogs have always been very popular here. You can eat them with one hand."

"We found a furnished rental house, too," Phillip admitted.

"For how many more days?"

"Through the end of the year?" Phillip said.

Spencer was quiet for a moment. "If you don't know what you're searching for then how do you know when you've found it?" he asked.

"You just know?" Phillip guessed.

"Are you just giving in to Mom here? Even though she's dead?"

"I have no idea what I'm doing," Phillip said. "It's like the old *Treasure Hunt* TV show, where at the end somebody dug frantically on a fake sand beach for a box of full of prizes."

"That was actually *Treasure Isle*, not *Treasure Hunt*. *Treasure Hunt* was even dumber. Contestants just picked a box, without even any clues or questions, to win money. But speaking of Isles, Trisha and I are headed for the Emerald Isle—that's Ireland—before Christmas. That's my news."

"I know what the Emerald Isle is," Phillip said.

"We were thinking of living there for a while anyway . . ." Spencer said.

"I see," Phillip said, because he did. "But that seems like a long way to go just to avoid the Chinese food."

CHAPTER SEVEN

Villa Villekula

SPENCER HOSTED THANKSGIVING AT his Soho loft for the four of them—it was only their second Thanksgiving without their mother, but Spencer and Trisha cooked all the foods that Jenny would have made. Spencer wore a sleek apron that read, "Kiss the Cook," but the "C" in Cook had been crossed out and replaced with an "M" so that it really read, "Kiss the Mook."

Places were set on the old Irish wake table that Spencer had bought years earlier at an antique store in the Adirondacks. He put out the plates decorated with blue cornflowers that he'd inherited from Jenny; Waterford tumblers beside modern polka-dotted champagne flutes for a pre-dinner toast; napkins of Irish linen that Trisha provided. The table featured a centerpiece of a hollowed pumpkin spilling fresh wildflowers. The whole room smelled of roasted turkey and buttery potatoes and Brussels sprouts braised in duck fat.

When they were ready to sit, Trisha noticed the fifth plate setting and asked, "Who's not here yet?"

"Oh, that's for Elijah," Spencer said.

"Who's that then, a friend of the family?" Trisha asked, already suspecting befuckery.

"Elijah the prophet," Spencer said.

"Are we leaving a seat for him at Thanksgiving now, too?" Phillip asked.

"Well we didn't have a Seder this year," Spencer said. "I figured we owe him a meal. Plus everyone else always feeds him in the spring. He probably doesn't get out much in autumn."

Phillip had to explain all of this to Trisha, while Spencer smiled like an eejit.

"There's an old Jewish tradition when we have the Seder—that's

36

the meal on the first night of the Passover holiday, celebrating the Jews' escape from slavery in Egypt," Phillip said. "This was back in the Cretaceous. Elijah protected us from the ten plagues that God perpetrated on our Egyptian captors—frogs; lice; boils; pestilence; John Tesh music; and so on. At the Seder we leave a seat for Elijah and open the door for his spirit to enter, expressing our trust in God's protection."

Trisha said. "I didn't suppose it had anything to do with Thanksgiving. It's like the Cowboys and the Indians, right?"

"The what?" Phillip asked.

"The footie," Trisha said. "Don't the Cowboys play the Indians in the footie every Thanksgiving?" She said it like "Tanks-giving."

"Oh, the football game," Phillip said, laughing. "No, it's the Cowboys and the Lions every year."

"Cowboys against *Lions*," she said. "You're joking. How is *that* a fair fight?"

At some point it had already become impossible to tell who was putting who on anymore.

"One more thing about Elijah," Spencer added. Most Jews don't know that he also shows up at circumcisions. Men are supposed to be circumcised to enjoy the Seder meal, and Elijah is like the penis police."

"Amen, then," Phillip said hoping it might shut his brother up. They clinked glasses, making sounds like text messages arriving.

"We beseech God to pour his wrath upon our oppressors," Spencer added.

When they'd served up the copious food and their mom's silver clattered on their mom's plates as they enjoyed her recipes, Spencer said, "Wayback Playback . . . Remember when we'd have Thanksgiving dinners at Aunt Phyllis and Uncle Jerry's house—you know, back when we thought Jerry was just our mean, dysfunctional uncle, before we learned he was also my mean, dysfunctional, lying father?"

Phillip wondered where this was going. Nowhere good, he thought.

Spencer turned to the wives.

"One year Mom brought along someone she described to us as 'a colleague.' Alan, I think it was, or Albert, or maybe Alvin—he did have a high voice like a chipmunk now that I think of it.

"Anyway, for whatever reason, Uncle Jerry took an immediate

dislike to him. Maybe he thought Alvin was sleeping with Mom and, well, *he'd* wanted to sleep with Mom—Uncle Jerry, that is. As you know, that's more or less how they created the miracle of me.

"Throughout the meal, whatever this guy said, Jerry contradicted him. I remember them talking about music. Alvin was crazy for jazz. He went on and on about Trane and Bird, like he knew them. It would have been annoying to anyone."

Spencer deepened his voice to imitate their uncle—and his father. "'It's music for children,' Jerry said. 'It's infantile. Purely tonal. No structure. They can't even write it down.'

"So Alvin changed the subject to movies. He'd just seen *One Flew Over The Cuckoo's Nest*. 'It was brilliant,' Alvin reported. He called it 'a new paradigm,' which if you think about it now was probably prescient of him. He said Jack Nicholson was someone to watch.

"Which is when Jerry asked him if he was an anarchist.

"Mom and Aunt Phyllis busied themselves clearing the plates and then basically hid in the kitchen, whispering. I thought they were planning a surprise of some kind, maybe a special dessert, or presents for us. Then I realized they were strategizing how to shut Jerry up. They sent me and Phillip and Leah into the den to play Scrabble.

"Leah set the game up on the coffee table and told us it was her house so we had to play by her rules. And her main rule was that obscenities counted double.

"It was hard to concentrate because we were trying to listen to what was going on in the dining room. The two men sat at opposite ends of the table and their voices were rising as we started to fill up the Scrabble board with words like 'fuck' and 'blowjob' and 'titties,' and 'mofo,'—which there was some discussion about, as to whether it was an abbreviation or a word itself.

"The whole thing was classic Leah: provocative and so wrong. We were like eleven and nine years old. She was laying the groundwork for a lifetime of rebellion. Even at that age she knew exactly who she was.

"Alvin was the first adult to come into the room where we were playing. He looked at the board and barked out a huge laugh. When Uncle Jerry came over to see what the jazz-loving anarchist was laughing at, he exploded. He kicked the table over. Even though it was a violent act he did it in what I can only describe as a girly manner. It revealed everything we ever needed to know about Uncle Jerry.

"Tiles flew everywhere and Leah crawled around on the floor trying to gather them up. Alvin got on his knees and helped. Leah was mortified. Mom and Aunt Phyllis were mortified. Alvin stood up with a tight smirk on his face and we thought there might be a fistfight. Then Uncle Jerry retreated to his bedroom. We anticipated the loud slamming of the door but he shut it gently, with great purpose. We didn't see him again for the rest of the night.

"It was quiet on the ride home. Phillip and I sat in the back, waiting for something. An excuse. An apology. For our mother to spin a story explaining that Jerry was under so much pressure at work and sometimes it got the better of him, or that he was ill, or worried about the Vietnam War, whatever.

"But she didn't say a word, and neither did Alvin. Phillip and I looked at each other thinking: someone's going to say something eventually—they're adults, they *have* to.

"Mom was driving, and she pulled up to a large house in Woodmere to drop off Alvin. We still had no idea who he was, what he did, what his relationship to Mom was, although we knew that 'colleague' was a euphemism—even though we didn't know what a euphemism was. We thought maybe he was a spy, although that's what we used to say about Uncle Jerry. Maybe they were opposing spies and that's why they'd had a fight.

"Alvin climbed out of the car and started walking up toward the house. We all watched him. When Mom dropped someone off she always waited to make sure they got into the house—as if kidnappers or aliens were lurking to steal them away. When he was nearly at the front door, Alvin turned around and came back down the driveway.

"He stopped by my car door. He motioned for me to roll down my back window. I thought he was going to punch me. I lowered it just enough so that we could hear him.

"'You spelled *fellatio* wrong,'" he said. 'In the Scrabble game. It has two ls.' Then he turned around again and walked to the house."

Spencer looked around the table.

Trisha erupted in what sounded like a laugh but nobody else was sure.

"It was the best line I ever heard anyone say," Spencer added. "It was like a Zen koan and I was suddenly enlightened. I wasn't sure of exactly what, but something was revealed to me. I felt I'd solved something intricate that had been hanging over me."

A few moments went by without anyone speaking.

"Well that's a heartwarming story," Phillip eventually said.

"It's a perfect tiny snow globe of our lives growing up," Spencer went on. "Mom and Phyllis covering for Uncle Jerry. Him acting like the misogynistic asshole he was. Leah churning the whole thing into her own irreverent artwork, us watching it like a movie that we were outside of. Like a combination of *Lord of the Flies* and *Pippi Longstocking*, where the pirate father goes missing and Pippi lives with a monkey and somebody breaks the smart kid's glasses, but instead of killing anyone, Pippi uses techniques of conflict resolution but they burn the whole island down anyway."

"And you're telling us this because why?" Phillip asked.

"Because, well, I have no idea why," Spencer said. "Maybe because it's Thanksgiving and that's our family Thanksgiving story. Maybe it proves that you can find revelation pretty much anywhere. Maybe because I like to say 'fellatio.'"

While they were sipping glasses of port after dinner and looking out the large windows at the lights of lower Manhattan, Spencer said, "I guess we won't be seeing each other much for a while."

He was referring to his and Trisha's imminent departure for Ireland, Phillip and Marty's return to Portland—though Spencer still believed this was a phase his brother was going through and it would work itself out in short order, whether he discovered the kind of secret their mother had referenced or not.

"While we're still together why don't we all just name one thing we're thankful for? Like normal families do?" Spencer suggested.

"Why don't you start," Phillip said, to test whether Spencer was setting up a gag.

Spencer, for his part, had actually given this some thought. "Sure, I'll start. Truth," he said. "I'm thankful for truth. For knowing what we know now, about where we came from. And where we're going—wherever that might be. And for the time and freedom to be able to learn the truth. So may we find what we're looking for, I guess is what I'm saying."

"What are you looking for?" Marty asked.

"Okay, let me change that. May we find *out* what we're looking for. And then may we find it. And may we leave it behind so someone will know that we were here. And that we found it. And left it behind."

Phillip nodded, still half waiting for a punch line. But his brother was done.

"I'm thankful for second chances," Marty said. She left it at that.

"Family," Trisha said. "The one that raised me—the normal and balanced one—and the new one I married into, with all its concomitant befuckery."

Phillip felt pressure. How could he compete with "concomitant befuckery?" He started to tear up, then choked it back. "I guess, well, Mom," he said. "And her legacy. Despite all the misdirection she did the best she could. We came out okay. At least I did. She knew what she was doing."

And with that, partly to close this at a natural endpoint and partly to prevent his brother's further blubbering, Spencer held up his glass of port. It reflected the sparkle of light beyond the window.

"Cheers," Phillip said.

"Yes, cheers," Marty repeated. "And thanks for bringing us together tonight. It was brave of you." She took Phillip's hand.

"Sláinte," Trisha added.

"Nostrovia," Spencer said, without having any idea why.

Part Two

Jenny

Chapter Eight

Thutmose III

For Phillip and Spencer's mother, Jenny Bernstein, conscious memory began at the Brooklyn Museum in 1949. Even much later, when dementia blunted her memories in the last year of her life at age seventy-four, she recalled looking up on a crisp October afternoon—hand in hand with her father—at the five mysterious doors topped by six pillars, all in the grand Beaux-Arts style. The clean lines of the gleaming marble awoke something. She was six years old and insisted they go inside, where she promptly fell asleep on the cold marble floor in front of the statue of Isis Nursing Horus—ironically, a representation of a devoted mother, which she was occasionally cogent enough to recall near the end with some pride given the successes of her own two wacky boys.

When she was eight Jenny's father Samuel bought her a membership to the museum—he remembered visits to the Kunsthistorisches Museum in Vienna from his own youth, and how the paintings had transported him to another world. At thirteen Jenny was allowed to go to the museum after school if someone walked with her—usually her brother Noah, a year younger but already a confident imp and a natural dry comedian whom people loved to be around. Noah was funny from the day their parents brought him home from Brooklyn Jewish Hospital with an admonition from Dr. Wolfe, the OB/GYN, who said the boy had come out of his mother laughing, and they should keep an eye on him.

At the museum Noah would gallantly kiss her hand and bid her adieux, off to play stickball in the street while their older sister Phyllis went, well, who knew where she went after school, since she didn't want to be seen with either of her siblings. In her mind Noah was still about six years old (and any time she mentioned her brother later in life she ascribed a much larger age difference), and Jenny was bookishly uncool—neither of which was true. Phyllis was probably off to paint her toenails and complain about homework and other inequities in the world in her buzz saw voice.

Once her brother dropped her at the museum, Jenny would greet the African-American guard in the grey uniform with a singsong, "Hello, Clarence!" on her way to the Egyptian exhibit. It wasn't lost on her that Clarence held some resemblance to the black marble statue of Senwosret III, and Jenny entertained the possibility that reincarnation might be ironic.

"Here to see Hor, Jenny?" Clarence would ask. "He's been very quiet today."

Hor was one of the mummies in the antiquities collection. His cartonnage—Clarence taught her the word for the papyrus covering that protected the wrapped body—was painted with brightly colored deities with the heads of foxes and birds and other animals. There were other humans, too. After Jenny told her family about this over the roast chicken at dinner one night, Noah drew her a colorful picture the next week in art class at school. His own primitive renderings were not so different from those made by the Egyptians, although he included depictions of the wrappers of some of Jenny's favorite candies—like Mary Janes, which Noah claimed tasted like peat moss—and images of Disney's Cinderella and Alice in Wonderland, and a tiny portrait that might have been Mr. Ainsworth, the math teacher from school.

"Hor's probably sad," Jenny reasoned to Clarence. "Because his wife was bitten by an asp."

"Or because somebody robbed his grave," Clarence offered.

Jenny waited for it.

"You know—he was surrounded by Thebes." Clarence had a smooth comic delivery. He never paused for the laugh. "Cleopatra had an asp too," he added, walking Jenny to her favorite room. "Or the asp had her, depending on how you look at it."

"Yes, the deadly villain, the poor, poisonous fool," Jenny said, quoting Shakespeare.

Jenny would read all the interpretive materials beside the displays of artifacts until she'd memorized them. She would sit on the floor in front of the wall reliefs of Nespeqashuty and do her homework, happy to be near these objects. She'd go to the museum library, intent on discovering something nobody else had figured out yet. She loved the story about how Howard Carter stumbled upon the burial site of King Tut just as his supporters were about to stop funding him. It taught her tenacity, particularly when confronted with difficult puzzles.

How was it possible that these items housed in this impressive structure in Brooklyn, New York, near Grand Army Plaza and the Botanical Gardens and her own home, were thousands of years old? And that they'd been lost for centuries and only rediscovered recently? And if that were true, what else had yet to be discovered? It wasn't only the things, but the *finding* of the things that awoke something in Jenny and built into her love of quests and mysteries, and the idea that places existed still on this earth that were redolent with the unknown. Which taught her to be excited by the world. And eventually incited traveling.

One afternoon when Jenny was fourteen and a light dusting of snow was settling on Brooklyn, she focused on the papyrus remnants of the Book of the Dead of the Goldworker of Amun, a hallmark of the museum's collection. She believed if she stared at it long enough the ancient writings would reveal their secrets to her. If humans had created the text and figures, she as a human, with proper attention, ought to be able to decipher their message across the millennia. She stared relentlessly until the figures squirmed and shifted. She feared ancient curses but determined the discoveries would be worth it. She considered whether Howard Carter's benefactor, Lord Carnarvon, had died as a result of such a curse, as some of the old newspapers she read suggested. An infected mosquito bite killed him just two months after the opening of Tut's tomb. Which taught her both caution and superstitiousness. Standing beside the tomb just before Carter became the first human to look inside the burial chamber of the child king in thirty-three centuries, Lord Carnarvon had asked, "Can you see anything?" and Carter answered: "Yes. Wonderful things."

But no flash of comprehension resulted from staring at the twenty-five-foot Book of the Dead scroll. No secrets were revealed. Although the scroll was purported to offer spells and advice to help the dead succeed in the afterlife, Jenny received no clear instruction.

What Jenny came to understand was that she and the Egyptians shared humanity. Which nurtured her lifetime love of adventure, of meeting people from other cultures and seeing things that were unimaginable: the pyramids, the Celsus Library at Ephesus, Hadrian's Wall in England, Angkor Wat and Machu Picchu, oceans of tulips in Holland and tortoises in the Galapagos Islands, the skyline of Hong Kong, macrons filled with raspberry jam in Paris, Mozart played in Vienna, Day of the Dead in Oaxaca, and on and on, marvelous, incomprehensible experiences, which taught her that above all else the world was full of sensual pleasures and the entirety of it was her home. Which eventually led her to want children to share it all with and reveal the world's secrets to. And maybe a husband, if that was absolutely necessary. But the last wasn't a requirement.

Chapter Nine
Desdemona

On the morning of the day that her brother Noah flew out of the back of the Bernstein family's produce truck on the Garden State Parkway with Jenny driving, she discovered a series of strange letters taped to the reverse side of the Alpha-Bits box at breakfast.

Jenny was eating alone, as she often did because she woke before the rest of the family. It was a September day full of promise, the sun still up early, the trees full of color, the neighbor's orange and black calico cat—named Mr. Tompkins—sitting primly on a lawn chair in the yard and staring into the house. Jenny waved to him through the picture window. Cats were considered Gods in Egypt, she mused. Best to be polite to them.

Jenny noticed the letters when she poured more milk into her cereal to create that sweet liquid at the bottom. She was startled, then amused, knowing only her brother could be behind this.

The stylized letters were familiar yet incoherent. They were meant to be hieroglyphics, she realized; something to be solved. Her brother knew how much she loved both puzzles and Egyptians, not to mention Egyptian puzzles. While she could almost make out the message some of the words didn't fully form.

It reminded Jenny of the lettering on her toothpaste tube in the reflection from the medicine cabinet mirror when she brushed her teeth. She carried the cereal box into the bathroom and held it up to the mirror. The letters arranged themselves into coherence, although it took her a moment to realize that the words had been separated in such a way as to make nonsense words until the spaces between them were also shifted.

THETO MBO FKING TOTIS
LO CATE DINT HEYAR DOF
BACKTEN PA CESFRO MT
HEPOLE OFT HELINE OFCLO THES
WON DER FULT HING SAW AITYOU

She said slowly, out loud, "The tomb of King Tot . . . is located in the yard of back . . . ten paces from the . . . pole of the . . . line of clothes . . . wonderful things await you . . ."

Line of clothes? She looked out into the backyard—the "yard of back"—which the cat had abdicated. There were no clothes in a line. But there was the clothesline.

She smiled at her brother's efforts to amuse her, particularly with the quote from Howard Carter. A few weeks earlier, when he dropped her at the museum, Noah had said, straight-faced, "You seem very wrapped up in mummies."

Was there something waiting for her in the yard? She would savor that question as a way of getting through the school day.

In the afternoon Jenny skipped the museum and came straight home. She was about to head outside to begin searching for whatever treasure Noah might have left for her when their father called them all into the parlor.

"A load of private tomatoes," he announced. "In New Jersey. Belmar." Samuel ran a produce business in lower Manhattan. He provided fruits and vegetables to the finest grocery stores and restaurants in New York, sometimes procuring them from as far away as Pennsylvania from a select group of farmers and orchardists.

"Isn't it late for tomatoes?" their mother asked.

"Precisely," Samuel said. "Our restaurants will be happy to have them! Our housewives will joyfully put them in salads or slice them on their bacon sandwiches with mayonnaise—one last hint of summer."

"I'll go," Noah said.

"You'll all go," their father said. "We'll find some fresh apple cider. A pie. It's a beautiful day. We'll swim in the ocean if it's warm enough."

"I'll ride in the back," Noah said. He loved to huddle in the back of the truck. Jenny suspected he imagined himself a soldier heading to liberate some European city, a humble worker or political activist, or some other heroic figure that only her brother could conjure.

"I'll drive," Jenny said. She was half kidding, although some of her older friends were already taking driver's education at school. Sometimes Samuel let one of the kids drive in an empty parking lot in the suburbs on Long Island. Phyllis was especially unskilled and had a short attention span, and Jenny and Noah would hug each other in the back seat, yelling while she gripped the wheel like a turret gunner.

As an immigrant, it wasn't odd to Samuel for his children to learn this important skill early. It was an acceptable violation of protocol.

"You can drive," he told Jenny. "Just don't mention to your mother."

"I'll stay home and do something interesting," Phyllis complained, knowing that she would go with them anyway.

"Are you still thinking of building that geodesic dome? Or working on your rocketry project?" Noah joked, and Phyllis threw a pencil eraser at him. Noah was the only human currently residing on planet Earth who could elicit Phyllis's nearly desiccated playfulness.

They piled into the old Ford with their father at the wheel, Jenny and Phyllis on the far side of the gearshift. Noah sat huddled in his pea coat in the bed of the truck.

When they'd crossed the Verrazano Bridge, but before they reached the Garden State Parkway, Samuel pulled over at a roadside rest area to change drivers. He breathed deeply standing beside the vehicle. The American dream stretched before him: clean air (well, for New Jersey) on a beautiful fall day, his own Ford F100, his children helping him work. He thought of his wife at home preparing something delicious for dinner, after which the kids would disappear to their various corners to complete homework assignments, embarked upon becoming good citizens, and successful.

It was a different time, and Jenny would become defensive later on when Phyllis wondered how Samuel let her drive at age fifteen, how he allowed his son to ride in the open bed of the truck.

As they motored along in the slow right hand lane of the Parkway with Jenny at the wheel, another truck over-full with apples hit something in the road and blew a tire. The sudden jolt of that vehicle launched a cascade of red delicious over the back rim. At sixty miles an hour the apples were perfect bombs. The first one shattered the windshield in front of Samuel and caused Jenny to squeeze the wheel with fury. Several flew over the top of their pickup. As three more bounded right at her, Jenny swerved hard out of her lane at the very moment that Noah stood up in the back of the truck, delighted by the rain of apples, ready to catch any that flew past.

He went over the tailgate with an impish grin as if embarking upon some great adventure.

CHAPTER TEN

Suicide King

WHEN NOAH WAS TWELVE he learned a card trick from Viktor, an old friend of Samuel's from Vienna, who first made Noah swear that he would never perform the trick more than once to the same audience, and that he wouldn't give away its secret. Then Viktor showed it to Noah, who fell down on the floor, yelling.

"The next time I see you I will teach you how it works," Viktor said in his Austrian accent. His big hands disappeared the cards back into the pocket of his overcoat, exposing a glimpse of the tattooed numbers on the insides of his wrists.

Noah wouldn't stop talking about the trick for a week. He considered the different ways in which it could have worked.

Maybe the entire deck consisted of the same card, or he was in some other way coerced to pick the nine of clubs. Maybe Viktor had communicated some code over the telephone even though the old man simply asked if he could speak to Mr. Wizard, and then asked Mr. Wizard to tell Noah his card.

Noah obsessed about it to his sisters, who stopped listening. Phyllis, especially, was uninterested in a stupid card trick. But it was more than that to Noah: it was a gateway to a world in which things operated according to mystical principles. It was the world he tried his whole short life to inhabit.

When Viktor next came to the house some months later he revealed the secret of Mr. Wizard, which was clever but a disappointment—until Noah performed the trick for Jenny and Phyllis. Even Phyllis forgot to be cynical and spent some of her precious, limited energy theorizing how it worked. Noah began carrying a deck of cards with him wherever he went. He became an acolyte for Mr. Wizard, spreading the joy and wonder while making sure not to perform it in front of the same people. And when the trick was over and a silent, smiling awe filled whatever room he was in, Noah would pocket the cards and refuse to discuss it.

But one day he offered to teach it to Jenny—Viktor had allowed that Noah could show it to one person after a period of time had elapsed.

―――――――――――

During Noah's shiva—the week-long Jewish gathering to remember the newly dead and comfort their loved ones—Jenny performed the trick publicly for the first time with the house full of relatives and neighbors and her parents' friends.

As the family sat in a tight caul of shock and pain in the living room, Jenny spoke in a newly forthright voice.

"Pick a card," she said to their kindly, nosy, widowed neighbor, Mrs. Silberman, on the third evening. The adults had finished with the sandwiches and moved on to coffee and rugelach. Some of the men were drinking Chivas Regal from paper cups.

Mrs. Silberman looked around the room. "Jennifer. Honey," she whispered hoarsely, although everyone could hear her. "You're not supposed to play games during shiva."

"It's not a game," Jenny said. "It's Noah's trick. He's going to speak to us from where he is now."

"Okay, sweetie," she said. She picked a card from the deck.

"Now show it to everyone," Jenny said.

Mrs. Silberman held up the king of hearts. Which was how Jenny began thinking of her dead brother: as the monarch with the knife to his head. Noah had always been the ruler of her heart.

Jenny picked up the phone and dialed a local number. "I'd like to speak with . . . Mr. Wizard," she choked into the phone. "Yes, I can hold."

Tears squeezed out of the corners of Jenny's eyes. "Hello, Mr. Wizard? Please tell Mrs. Silberman her card."

She offered the black receiver to Mrs. Silberman, who considered the other adults watching her. Mrs. Silberman held the phone up so the rest of them could hear. A deep male voice said, "Your card is the king of hearts. Please tell Jenny to do good, keep her heart light, and Osiris will reunite us in the Field of Reeds."

Mrs. Silberman dropped the phone and sat back on the couch with both hands on the seat cushions. Jenny thought the final salutation was a fine dramatic flourish, and exactly like something her brother would have said.

What Jenny did not mention was that to her, Mr. Wizard was the thing that would keep Noah alive. The trick became his legacy, and many years later she would teach it to her own children without them ever knowing it was her way of continuing to shepherd her brother through the afterlife. It was Noah's own book of the dead, and explained why Jenny had slipped a deck of cards into her dead brother's pocket at the funeral home when nobody was looking.

Later in the week, when visitors began to wane and the family was looking at what life might be like going forward, Jenny remembered the message on the back of the cereal box. She retrieved the box from the kitchen and carried it into the bathroom to hold it up to the mirror again. When she emerged, Phyllis was standing in the kitchen, arms crossed, her hair newly pouffed.

"Why are you eating cereal in the bathroom?" she asked.

Jenny shook her head. "I got a message. From Noah."

"I don't know why he taught *you* that card trick," Phyllis said. Jenny knew Phyllis wished it was her who'd flown out of the back of the truck. She suspected her sister blamed her for the accident.

"Because he loved me," Jenny said.

When Phyllis stomped off to school—she wanted to go to school now that she saw herself as a tragic figure who'd lost her dear brother—and their parents walked down the street toward shul, Jenny feigned going to school herself but then circled back to the empty house.

She took down a shovel from where it hung on a rusty nail in the garage and headed to "the yard of back." Mr. Tompkins, the cat, was waiting for her. He mewled twice in greeting—or warning.

Jenny wondered: could the hieroglyphics Noah left her inadvertently have come with a curse, and by her mere willingness to break the code she'd incurred the wrath of some vengeful Egyptian god who killed her brother? Was Mr. Tompkins involved in all this, since the Egyptians had worshipped and feared cats and their magical powers?

If either or both of these things were so, perhaps the Egyptians were also right about the afterlife. Maybe her brother was traveling homeward to some eternal paradise—to the Elysian Fields—where he would live in great peace and harmony, knowing the world's greatest secrets; certainly he was still communicating with her. She just needed to discover what he'd left her in the yard of back, ten paces from the pole of the line of clothes.

She approached the dig mathematically. She'd read enough tales of Howard Carter, and Charles Edwin Wilbour from the Brooklyn Museum, and other Egyptologists to know she needed a specific plan. First she looked for telltale signs of digging, but the yard had been uniformly mowed and raked to hide any obvious disturbances.

She measured out ten paces in each of four directions from each pole of the clothesline and drew dots in the grass with a can of black spray paint from the garage that her father had bought to cover dings on the produce truck. She took larger steps than were natural for her because she recognized her brother was taller, and his paces would be bigger than her own. It was a solution that Noah would have admired. Then she connected the dots into circles.

Part of one of the circles intersected the poured concrete patio slab; her brother wouldn't have buried anything under the slab. While he'd likely thought of it, he probably didn't have the time or resources. Which left her with one full circle and one partial circle with circumferences of about twenty feet.

Jenny began digging test holes at the four compass points in the first full circle. Her plan was to go down twelve inches, then fill in every two feet with another hole if the first four holes revealed nothing. If she dug all the holes around the perimeter without finding anything, she'd take each hole down another foot, then dig some more holes inward toward the center. If she didn't find anything by then she would reassess her plan.

She dug neatly, carrying the dirt one shovelful at a time to a growing pile in the corner of the yard beside her mother's rose bushes. She was as meticulous as a scientist, and as confident as a bully: she knew her brother. All signs pointed to this. When a blister peeled back a layer of skin on her thumb and exposed a red welt, she reveled in the sting. It wasn't lost on her that she was digging something up shortly after they'd buried Noah.

Samuel and Eva came home from temple in the early afternoon, while Jenny was taking a break from her excavations. She was leaning on the shovel in the backyard with a glass of iced tea in one hand.

"What is this you are doing in the dirt?" her father asked, and the glass slipped through her fingers and shattered on the ground.

"Jenny?" her mother asked, as if from a long way off. "Jennifer? Are you ho-kay?"

"I'm fine," Jenny said. "I'm looking for something. Noah left it for me."

Her parents considered each other with raised eyebrows. They surveyed the yard, polka-dotted with test holes. They noted the pile of dirt by the rose bushes.

"He left me a secret message. On the back of the Alpha-Bits box."

Their exchange of concerned expressions was not lost on her. "Before he died," she clarified. "A puzzle. A game. He was sending me on a quest. He was trying to reveal a secret to me."

Jenny marched past them up the back steps and into the kitchen. She retrieved the cereal box from the cupboard. But the hieroglyphics were gone.

"Phyllis must have taken it," Jenny said. "She was jealous. Noah didn't teach her Mr. Wizard."

"Darlink girl," her father said. "Leave off with the shoveling. With the digging. There's nothing out here."

"How about some hot soup for you?" her mother asked. "A cup of Lipton with honey? Have you eaten anything? Did you not go to school?"

"Mother. That's too many questions. Please. I know what I'm doing. Give me a few more hours. Humor me."

"I am going to call Dr. Blaustein," Samuel said. "He can give you something to relax your mind."

"My mind is fine," Jenny said, which at that point—and for nearly another sixty years—still held true.

———————

Jenny snuck back out to the yard in the night, after everyone else had gone to sleep. She dug quietly, pushing the shovel down with the heel of her snow boot, leaning her weight on the handle so the blade pried up the turf and the fine, dark soil. She dug in the ambient glow from a streetlight and the sconce on a neighbor's porch. In her flowered flannel nightgown and fall coat.

Still, Phyllis heard her and crept down the back stairs and through the kitchen and into the yard. She stood in her own lace-collared nightgown, one hand on a hip. Her face was darkened by a mud beauty mask that made her look sinister.

"Why did you take the message off the Alpha-Bits box," Jenny asked.

"I don't know what you're talking about," Phyllis said. "Mother and father say you're bereaved. You're not yourself. You're not thinking straight."

"The message was for me," Jenny said. "You know that."

"He taught me the card trick, too," Phyllis said. "I know how it works."

"Okay," Jenny said, uncertain whether she believed her sister.

"He taught it to me first. He loved me, especially," Phyllis said.

"He loved everyone," Jenny said. "Even you. He couldn't help himself."

Toward morning Jenny discovered the burial chamber of King Tot. It was close to hole C at a depth of fifteen inches, down to twenty-four inches. The sides of the pit had been reinforced with plywood. Noah had buried a cigar box—H. Upmann Coronas Minor Tubos—painted with bright blues and reds and yellows depicting crude deities. A cuneiform man with a sparrow's head. A woman with the head of a sphinx. Jackals and brick pyramids, all painted in tiny, colorful detail on the outside of the box. A rendering of a house that looked like their own. Some of the images were covered in silver foil that Jenny recognized as the wrappers from Hershey's Kisses.

Inside the cedar box was a paper mache cartonnage, which had been pushed down so that when she slid the wooden cover off the box the cartonnage popped out as if spring-loaded. It was painted with a doll's face and jeweled necklaces and dazzling rings and bracelets: oddly, the main figure appeared dressed in a powder-blue stewardess's uniform.

Jenny thought further of Egyptian curses and poor Lord Carnarvon, dead of that infected mosquito bite on his ass not long after his money helped Howard Carter exhume King Tut. If she wasn't so certain this was a message from her brother she might have thrown it all back in the hole and covered the relics over again with dirt.

Beneath the cartonnage in the cigar box was a figure wrapped in gauze bandages that she knew came from the first aid shelf in the house—last used when Phyllis had scraped her knee falling off her bike and had wailed for about two hours. As Jenny carefully unrolled the bandages she recognized the British Airways stewardess doll that her Aunt Liza had brought her years ago from a trip to Europe. The doll had come to represent freedom and adventure, and Jenny would think of it often in later years as she developed her business as a travel agent.

Beneath and around the stewardess lay a collection of tiny doll-sized grave goods: cooking utensils from other dolls Jenny had given up years ago; the peanut butter flavored candies that were her favorite; a few toy soldiers to protect the cache from grave robbers. Two Cracker-Jack rings and one actual silver ring with a tiny blue gemstone etched with lines of gold: lapis lazuli, she recognized—beloved by the ancients. Jenny knew that nearly all Egyptians, from peasants to pharaohs, wore jewelry. She had no idea where Noah procured this, or with what money. She put it on immediately—it was too big for her ring finger so Jenny wore it on her thumb. As time went by and she grew, Jenny moved the ring to subsequently smaller fingers, until it no longer fit on her pinky during the hot, swollen summer of the year she was eighteen.

Chapter Eleven
The Book of Two Ways

Phyllis quickly moved on from the death of their brother—leading Jenny to wonder whether, like an Egyptian mummy, her sister's heart had been removed and placed in a jar. Jenny sunk deeper into despair the longer Noah was gone from them.

She channeled her energies into her study of Egyptology. She lived her life in a shadowed triangle between school, home, and the Brooklyn Museum. Her room piled with books about the First Dynasty, The Valley of the Kings, and Jean-Francois Champollion's quest to decipher the Rosetta Stone. Jenny deep-dove into Duat, the Egyptian world of the dead. She read the tragic letters that Lady Duff Gordon wrote home when she was dying in Egypt and begged her British husband not to come back for her.

Jenny considered the concepts of permanence and change, and that knowledge was the key to resurrection. Egyptology convinced her that we are still connected to those who've passed on, and that we always will be—something that stayed with Jenny for a lifetime. She also knew that the living were responsible to ensure that their dead loved ones survived into eternity. At the end of her own time on earth, Jenny would remember her studies as "having lived in ancient Egypt."

Samuel and Eva became concerned when Jenny chose to read at home or visit the museum yet again on the weekends rather than joining her friends when they gathered for parties or to listen to new record albums. She showed no interest in the boys who came around for a while and then came only for her sister.

When this had gone on for several months and the psychiatrist they'd insisted on could make no diagnosis, something had to be done. To be fair, Samuel and Eva also had trouble shaking the pallor that had settled over their lives—which was like watching a black and white television show: familiar actions had definition but lacked any splash of color, any verve. The door to Noah's room remained closed.

One night at dinner Samuel announced that he was selling the house.

"Whaaat? Will we live on the street?" Phyllis asked in a panic.

"Yes. In the car," Samuel said. "We'll tie a mattress on the roof for you and your sister."

"We've bought another house," their mother said with manufactured cheerfulness. "A new house. On Long Island."

Eva tried to look animated but failed. Samuel's own buoyancy was only half faked in comparison—this was something he'd mentioned every now and again for years. A move to Long Island, among Brooklyn Jews, was a sign of true arrival—beyond the original arrival of Ellis Island, which was something, but not the realized promise of America that immigrants imagined as they packed their belongings in the debris of Europe in the 1940s.

"Long Island?" Phyllis screeched. "We don't know anybody on Long Island! After all this you're going to take our home away from us?"

Jenny remained taciturn. Her first thought was that she would be separated from the museum—her own real home. Her second thought was to recognize that was precisely the reason they were moving.

Jenny became a cheerleader at her new high school in Hewlett because it was the opposite of everything she'd been before. It was what all the prettiest girls did. Her parents rationalized that she was emerging as something else, and thought it a good sign.

Jenny recognized that if she surrounded herself with other high school students her family would have a harder time seeing that she had not recovered from the death of her brother. Teenaged girls were the perfect camouflage—although boys still seemed dangerous because they might want to know her. Jenny was distraught enough not to care, so she committed herself to outward cheerfulness despite remaining deeply depressed. It was an application of her life-long practice of misdirection—first learned from the Mr. Wizard trick that Noah taught her—and it worked. Jenny did not seek out friends that year, yet made many because she was exotically beautiful and soft spoken and kind in an effort to hide the darkness that obsessed her. On the field, her cheers were loudest, her leg kicks the highest. She shook her pom-poms with manic ferocity.

Phyllis adopted the opposite strategy, ultimately surrounding herself with boys who could take her mind off the death of her brother. She was a senior that year and still bitter about not getting to spend the rest of high school in Brooklyn. At first, on weekends, Phyllis took a complex combination of mass transit back to the old neighborhood, which she would not let go of, and so she made few friends in their new home. Then, when the travel became wearying, she went out on dates every weekend.

Samuel and Eva drove to the fruit warehouse in Brooklyn most mornings before even the devoutest commuters began their day, and were back in the early afternoons before the girls returned from school. Jenny determined they were like something from a science fiction movie, going through the motions of parenthood despite being soulless beneath their exteriors. When she first saw *A Charlie Brown Christmas* some years later, she recognized the parents as her own: absent, making strange sounds that nobody could decipher. Samuel and Eva were pure background—providing food and a house and a tiny allowance, encouraging her to apply for junior college. But only definable through the impacts of their actions, entirely peripheral. They'd also disappeared inside themselves after Noah's death.

If she could get through the final two years of high school Jenny thought she could figure a way to move back to Brooklyn, to continue her studies at the museum.

But she didn't factor Jack Elliot into her precise calculations.

Chapter Twelve

Patrick Swayze

Jenny met Jerry Rothstein poolside at Kellerman's resort in the Catskills on a summer day that felt as hot and wet as a load of laundry just out of the washing machine. Jenny was reading in a chaise beside the turquoise water, the scent of chlorine both refreshing and nostalgic. The seat next to her—where Phyllis had been perched before her tennis lesson—was empty.

"That's a big book you're reading," Jerry said by way of introduction—even though it wasn't. He was bronzed to the color of Catskill Jews. He wore a gold chai around his neck on a thick gold chain and a heavy gold-link bracelet on his right wrist. He was hairy as a bear and his voice was deep and confident as he stood over her. His flat feet were gigantic, Jenny noticed, like he was wearing swim fins, except he wasn't.

"Yes, and it's full of big words," she said, moving her bent legs together until they touched.

"Good?" Jerry asked. When she looked at him blankly he added, "The book?"

"Well," Jenny said, picking up her bookmark, placing it between the pages, and closing the book to clutch it closer to her chest. "That depends on what you mean by 'good.'"

"Are you enjoying it?"

That too was a difficult question. It was Updike's *Rabbit Run*. Was that a book you could really enjoy? Reading about a loveless marriage of convenience where both spouses were trapped and unhappy, when their earlier lives had promised so much?

"Do you know Updike?" she asked.

"Not personally," Jerry said, smiling as if he'd just been clever. "Is he a Jew?" Which Jenny knew was his way of asking if she was a Jew.

As if anyone who wasn't a Jew would be sunbathing next to the pool at Kellerman's. There was something formal in his speech. An accent?

"Where are you from?" Jenny asked him.

"New York," he said, smiling as if this were funny.

"And before that?"

"The diaspora," he said, as if it were a country. "My parents are Sephardim. So, Spain two generations ago. With Ellis Island connecting the two."

"Why did you ask if Updike is a Jew?"

"Well, if his book is called *Rabbi, Run,* I figured he might be."

She laughed at that, and he nodded. She would realize later that what Jerry lacked more than any human she'd ever encountered was a sense of humor. If he was funny, it was inadvertent. If he was trying to be funny, it usually left people with quizzical looks.

"It's *Rabbit Run*. Like the cute animal with the pink nose," Jenny said.

"You're a cute animal," Jerry said. "But with a red nose. You've been out in the sun for too long, maybe," he added. "Maybe you'd like to go inside and have a drink and cool off."

She squinted up at his proffered hand. Her instincts warned her off but she'd hoped for the company of a man on this visit to Kellerman's with her parents and her sister. It's what they'd hoped for her, too. Even a boring man would be more interesting than dinner with her family. She aspired to go dancing some evening. And a drink sounded nice. A whiskey sour, icy and sweet. She was just sixteen, despite looking older, and a whiskey sour was the only cocktail she'd ever had.

"Maybe not right now," Jenny said, deferring a decision without discouraging him.

"An aperitif, then? Say at six o' clock. At the tiki bar." He smiled and she noticed his teeth were white and perfect against his dark complexion, and the way he tilted his head to the side when inviting her conveyed a boyish vulnerability. He was in his early twenties but acted like an old man, until he smiled. But there was something plastic about the entire presentation. He moved stiffly. He was a robot. Programmed for Catskill Jewyness.

———

Jenny was walking from the pool back to her and Phyllis's room to shower and maybe lay her head down for twenty minutes when she noticed Jack Elliot sitting on a concrete wall outside the back of the dining room, smoking. He waved with the two fingers that were holding the cigarette.

She smiled at him because it was the right thing to do, and because he was handsome, and because his wave was both familiar and casual simultaneously. He was the most—perhaps the only—non-Semitic thing she'd laid eyes on in days.

"You were at my table this morning," he said through an exhale of smoke. "You didn't finish your omelet. You drank two glasses of orange juice and two cups of coffee. How do you like the Updike?"

"You were either my waiter or you need a hobby," she said.

He must have noticed the book at breakfast since her arms were currently draped over the cover. "It's so tragic," she said, opening up to him like, well, the pages of a book.

"And so funny at the same time," he said. "I played sports in school but if that's going to be the highlight of my life I'll write a book called *Rabbit, Jump*, because I'd jump off a building."

He stubbed the cigarette butt against the concrete wall and hopped down. "It's back to work for us Goyim," he said. He said it like he hadn't spoken the word before and was testing it out.

"What time are the Goyim finished working?" Jenny asked, surprising herself.

"Well . . . this one can be at the dock with a fresh thermos of Jameson and soda by, say, nine," Jack said. He didn't look up when he said it. There was no desperation in him, just a hopeful confidence that moved her. He was a boy, still, but might be a man tomorrow. He was handsome as a Kennedy, with square teeth and a hint of freckles, the short, sandy rough-cut hair of the working class.

Jenny brought Phyllis to the arranged rendezvous with Jerry Rothstein. Although their father had insisted, Jenny had her own reasons. At first Jerry appeared disappointed, then she could see him calculating that maybe his stock had gone up: two pretty girls to be seen with at the bar. At the very worst he'd look popular to anyone else who was watching.

He made a show of putting their drinks on his tab—Jenny ordered a wine spritzer, because she heard another woman ask for one, and it sounded so refreshing, and because nobody would be able to tell if it was a real drink, not that anyone would have cared at Kellerman's. At first she thought the woman had asked for a wine *shvitzer*, which caused Jenny to giggle to herself.

Phyllis ordered a Tanqueray and Tonic with three limes. Not a gin and tonic: Tanqueray. Jerry drank Dewar's, rocks. Jenny interpreted that as his own nod toward goyish sophistication. This gathering place of Jews was as remarkable for their desperation to assimilate as for their simultaneous need to prove their Hebraic bona fides. There were code words—a little Yiddish thrown in: "schmuck," "tsuris," an occasional "oy"; references to "the holidays," which meant Rosh Hashanah and Yom Kippur, not Thanksgiving and Christmas. They bragged on their Long Island home bases and their donations to Zionist causes. Jenny couldn't figure out if they were trying to appear more or less Jewish or both at the same time, but she wanted no part of it.

When Jerry dropped braggy references to Brandeis and 47th Street in a voice as deep as a Jewy ocean, Jenny put her plan into place. She was subtle: a hand on his arm for the briefest moment, a laugh at something he said that wasn't remotely funny. She looked into his eyes, but only when her sister was watching. When Phyllis moved her bar stool closer to Jerry's, Jenny knew the hook had been set.

"You two seem to be getting along swimmingly," she said, thinking in the back of her mind that they'd spend the day at the pool tomorrow. "I think I'll take a sandwich back to my room and read for a while."

Jerry's eyes followed her out of the bar, but Phyllis was watching Jerry.

Jenny skirted the dining room and picked up a sandwich from the snack bar. She didn't want to see Jack working his tables because the thrill of that felt too dangerous. She'd let him wonder where she'd gotten to, and whether she might show up at the dock at nine.

Back in her room—on the small bed, with the door open to the sound of crickets—she rampaged through the Updike. When she looked up it was 8:30 already—nearly dark, and she was still in her pre-dinner slacks. She hoped that Phyllis wouldn't come back to the room while she put on her makeup. Her sister had likely gone to dinner with Jerry, and maybe dancing after. Jenny wondered if he was waiting for the return of the younger, prettier sister, but making due with what was before him, a surer thing.

When she arrived at the dock—breathless, feeling the delicious tang of being a bad girl, which was new to her—Jack was leaning back in a blue rowboat with his feet up on the gunwale, smoking. He wore khaki trousers and a pair of Sperry Topsiders, like he'd just gotten off a yacht in Hyannis Port. Candles flared at the bow and stern. Jenny could see the shape of a pack of Marlboros in the rolled up sleeve of his white tee shirt. He was sipping from a plastic thermos cup. He sat up when he spotted her, putting his feet on the deck of the boat. She saw how the sight of her pleased him.

"Permission to come aboard, Captain," she said, standing on the dock, looking down at him.

"Permission granted," he said. He stood in the boat and took her hand. She felt the unsteadiness—both the boat's and her own.

"I was afraid you might not come," Jack said.

"And I've been afraid of showing up," she admitted.

"Shall we go out?" he asked, and she didn't understand at first that he meant in the boat, out on the lake.

"Aren't they all locked up for the night?"

"I know people," he said, smiling, and holding up a key. "We're already cleared for take off. That's a mixed metaphor, I'm aware," he said. "Which a college girl like you might notice."

She shook her head. "Not yet," she said. "I mean about college."

When she'd arranged herself on the wooden seat in the bow Jack pushed the boat away from the dock and took up the oars. The keel made low ripples in the dark lake water. Like corduroy. Like shaking out a bedspread. A sliver of moon floated upward above distant pines as the sky darkened. The sound of the boat moving in the water was quenching.

"Drink?" Jack said, indicating the thermos with his chin while he pulled on the oars carefully, quietly, not just with power but also with finesse, and she felt the boat shifting beneath her but carrying her along with it, which was also how, after that first drink, she felt about Jack.

He was from Long Island. He was done with high school and waiting to join the military, working for the summer because he liked working. She admitted she was finishing high school. Well, not really finishing but finishing the year before finishing.

"You look older," he said.

"I feel older."

"Why is that?"

"My brother died," Jenny said, although she'd had no intention of talking about Noah to anyone. "I killed him."

"I doubt that," Jack said. "You don't look like the murdering type."

She felt comfortable with Jack. Safe. She had no idea why. Which made him dangerous. He was the most natural man she'd ever encountered, and his Irishness was so raw and blatant that she was moved by him.

She started crying without any indication that it was coming on. She startled herself, which made her cry even harder.

"I assure you we're seaworthy," Jack said, leaning toward her, resting the oar handles under his thighs. He reached out a hand. "And I'm a junior lifeguard as well. So no need for that."

She grasped his fingers in her own. The boat's momentum slowed and he did not let go of her hand.

She told him the whole story about the hieroglyphics on her cereal box and the apples flying at her in the truck and even the Egyptian concept of the afterlife. Jack became in those moments Jenny's own Rosetta Stone, a key to understanding her circumstances. Like the Egyptians, she was also struggling to manage the relationship between permanence and change.

He told her it would get better with time. "Everybody loses someone," he said. "Everybody dies. You've got a long, happy life ahead of you . But it's okay to feel sad."

Why hadn't anyone else told her that? Jenny's heart cleaved open like a split watermelon, spilling her emotions like tiny black seeds until she was sure they would fill up the small boat and drown them both. It wasn't what she'd wanted, but she thought she could see a future with this man.

When she was done talking to Jack about Noah, Jenny never spoke of her brother to anyone other than Jack again.

Part Three

Phillip and Spencer

Chapter Thirteen

Pi

Back in Ireland after New Year's, ensconced in Trisha's stone cottage 1.7 kilometers from downtown Ballydraiocht (he measured it on his Fitbit when they returned, so he could know how much exercise he'd get walking to the village), Spencer eased into rural life. But after the second week he grew restless. He'd never lived in a small town before. Certainly not a small town in Ireland. With a new wife. And decent pizza thousands of miles away. If he was already annoyed by the notion that his dead mother had sent him on a quest, agita did not improve his mood.

He and Phillip had taken to Zooming each other on Sundays when it was nine a.m. in Portland and six in the evening in Ireland. Spencer thought of it as talking to his brother from the future. He wondered if there was a way to monetize it. Every week Spencer set a different background behind him on the call—the first that caught Phillip's attention was an underground scene from *The Lord of the Rings*, but where all the orcs had the face of Vladimir Putin.

"I've been going to the pub a fair amount," Spencer admitted one Sunday. "Purely as an anthropological investigation of local customs."

"Of course. You're probably not even drinking because that might interfere with your research."

"Not entirely correct, sir, but more or less," Spencer said. "I'd like to share a few observations with you."

"So secrets *have* been revealed to you."

"Let's start with darts," Spencer said, ignoring the deeper implication of his brother's inquiry. "The lads—I'm calling people 'lads' now—seem daft for it. I'm also using words like 'daft.' But I'm not sure I get it—the darts, that is. I noticed, for example, that the target's not even moving. Where's the sport in that? And they actually watch this on TV. The telly, I mean. It's like curling, but without the excitement of the sweeping. It's like if baseball only had someone in the outfield throwing the ball to second base. Over and over again."

"Is it possible you're not cut out for life as an Irish country squire?" Phillip asked.

"Trisha is so happy being home. So there's some joy in Mudville. When I said that, and then explained it to her, she accused me of going on about the baseball again."

"How's the band?" Phillip asked, attempting to change the subject and avoid a tirade about baseball.

"That's another thing. You know I have a little time on my hands. So I thought I'll manage the band since nobody else is doing it. I managed Tower of Haggis in New York for all those years, how hard could this be? I thought I'd find another gig for us to play. Or even a try out somewhere else to see whether the crowd liked us or threw potatoes at us.

"So I drove to the next town one day and talked to the owner of the pub there—it's a lot like the pub here—and he said sure, he'd give us a whirl. So when we had our next rehearsal I mentioned it to the band and the room went all quiet.

"'Oh, Spencer, we don't want another gig,' Joanie said," Spencer said in a falsetto voice with a deplorable Irish accent.

"'Bollox on more gigs,' Billy said," Spencer said in an equally bad male Irish voice.

"Bands are always troublesome. I get that," Phillip said. "But what about the good stuff?"

"The landscape is friggin' spectacular, and the Guinness is second to none. I'm playing golf twice a week and some of the guys I met in the clubhouse asked me to play poker with them some time. I'm reading a lot of books. I just finished *Finnegan's Wake*."

"There's no way you read *Finnegan's Wake*."

"I meant *Charlotte's Web*," Spencer said. "I'm also hiking out on the moops whenever the weather is clear."

"You mean the moors?" Phillip asked.

"'The correct answer is 'the moops,'" Spencer went on, delivering the *Seinfeld* line that his brother might have been the only other person in the world who would understand.

"You know that's a life most people would dream of," Phillip said.

"It must be the pizza then. For starters, there is none. Secondly, if they had it they'd probably put baked beans on it. I mean no disrespect to my Irish brothers, but how fucking hard would it have been to learn a few culinary skills in the past 2,000 years? Could they not have picked up something from the French?"

"And I miss Jews," Spencer continued. "Which I totally didn't see coming. Not going to temple and all that religious stuff, but the part where people buy bagels at Zabar's on Sundays and share their spiritual beliefs without actually having any!"

"Let's stay focused on the positive for a minute."

"The people are fantastic. And hilarious. And generous to a fault. They're great storytellers and warm and inclusive. They don't hate me—at least not yet—like most people learn to do. They accept me for the irreverent genius I am.

"I love Trisha more than I've ever cared for anything in my life. More than the New York Jets. More than Springsteen. More than I loved Shari Haberman in sixth grade when she let me put my hand up her shirt. Oh, and the curries: fantastic! But I'm still struggling here. It's just not home to me. I keep waiting for Mom's secret to be revealed, but so far . . .."

"I get it," Phillip interrupted.

"So I'm going to just try to let the love carry me through for a while. And the Guinness. How's Oregon? Do you feel this kind of ennui being in a new place far from home? Are you adrift in a small boat on a giant ocean, and your fellow passenger is a hungry tiger?"

"Portland is an experiment for me and Marty, too," Phillip said. "Every day is something new. I ate geoduck last week, and I don't even like the name, or the spelling of it, let alone that it looked like the world's biggest loogie. I rode a stand-up paddleboard. Which is a little like darts I guess since I just didn't get it.

"We take walks in this neighborhood full of beautiful old houses, especially in the evenings when the lights are on and we can see the people and their cats through the windows. Even the rain has become something I look forward to. I'm reading all the Booker Prize novels, which are terrific, except for the one about Bob Marley. We took a theater subscription—it's not Broadway, but still: they're so earnest! I spend hours in the bookstore and when I come out the air smells like fresh hops and mesquite-grilled meat. And there's a giant mountain that you can see from almost everywhere on the three days a year that it's clear."

"But don't you miss New York?"

"Of course I miss New York. I spent the first fifty-plus years of my life there. And I've only had fifty-plus. There's no subway here and they don't even have a daily newspaper. Some of the people are still living in the fifties—I mean the 1850s—given their political views. I know saying that makes me sound like you. The point is: it's different. I'm learning again. Every day some new shit happens and I find myself referring to Coke as 'pop' rather than 'soda' or I see an old man riding an electric bike or I eat an ice cream flavor like bone marrow that never would have occurred to me before—and for good reason. I'm saying hello to strangers I pass on the street rather than putting my hand on my wallet.

"But, like you, no revelations—which is one of the reasons I came here. Which makes me feel like maybe Mom played us for suckers. Or she was just totally out of it when she suggested this odyssey. But I'm still hopeful. I'm optimistic *something* will be revealed."

"You're optimistic. That's what you do," Spencer said. "Are you going to stay awhile? Optimistically?"

"I have no idea. We're just living every day waiting for the skies to cleave open and for God or some ancient Egyptian deity to speak to us. I've got this new real estate project—as you would know if you actually ever listen when I talk—so that keeps me busy for a few hours. Maybe you need an anchor like that."

"You're not suggesting I start working, for fuck's sake?"

"People do worse things."

"I'm unemployable. I have no skills. I don't like people. I don't get along with them. I got fired from my job delivering newspapers in junior high because I crossed out the headlines I didn't agree with. So work is out. And with nothing to do I'm not sure how long I can stay here."

"Why don't you think about your current situation as traveling, but just that you're doing it in one single place? You love to travel. Go see some castles, or something."

"I have no idea what that even means," Spencer said. "But when has that ever stopped me?"

Chapter Fourteen
Zayed bin Sultan Al Nahyan, et. al.

In Portland, Phillip and his new young partners focused on their renovation project in the eclectic Hawthorne neighborhood. Phillip had provided the capital from one of the real estate funds he managed. It was a small project by the standards of his deals of the past few years but a fine way to add some additional geographic diversity to the portfolio and give him something to do while he and Marty stayed in the Rose City.

Whenever Phillip walked through a building with a mind to buying and renovating it, he was brought back to the very first property he owned, when he was a junior at Vassar. He'd pitched the deal to his mother, who recognized his entrepreneurial talents from years of snow-shoveling and house-painting ventures as a boy. And what she'd taught him: the game-playing skills that comprised a major foundation of his talents.

As his final project for a business class sophomore year Phillip presented the concept that a student (him, for example) living off campus—say in a damp, drafty house along Raymond Avenue with a couch that had survived 1,000 keg parties—could earn free housing by taking the money he'd otherwise spend (or that his mother would) for two years of rent and fronting it as the three percent down payment on the purchase of said multi-bedroom house, that he could then rent to his friends, thereby paying no rent *and* having his roommates pay his mortgage.

"What if it doesn't work?" his mother had asked when he was home for Christmas break, trying to convince her to co-sign the loan.

"I'll sleep in the quad," Phillip said. "I'll shower at the gym and eat scraps out of the dumpster behind the dining room." He gave his mother that smile he knew she was powerless against.

"What if your kooky friends trash the place?" Jenny asked. "What if they mix Quaaludes and martinis and suddenly feel that all the furniture must be pushed out a second floor window?"

"Wait, I told you about that?" Phillip said.

Jenny could only shake her head. "This isn't going to be like when your brother asked for money for a science fair project and spent it on making pornography with that slut Stacey Shulman?"

"I am so not my brother," Phillip said, and they both knew how true that was.

———————

In early February Spencer was far more upbeat on the brothers' scheduled Zoom call. He was sitting out on the deck wearing a puffy coat and a watch cap with the Tayto Crisps logo. Phillip noted that the background revealed rolling green hills dotted with white blotches that could only be sheep or giant patches of suds from a dishwasher that had accidentally been filled with laundry soap. And it wouldn't have been the first time.

"Why so cheerful?" Phillip asked. Had Spencer received a revelation?

Spencer was silent for a moment, which Phillip recognized as a set-up for something.

"It's been a good week. We've been bringing in the sheeps." He paused, then added, "We did go rejoicing, bringing in the sheeps."

"I think you mean sheaves, although frankly I don't know what a sheave is."

"Still, we're rejoicing, and that's the main thing," Spencer said. Then he paused another perfect beat: "Should we not have brought in the sheeps?"

"Are you *really* rejoicing?"

"Actually, yes. I may be getting the hang of this whole Irish country living thing."

"How so?

"Well, like yesterday, for example. I got up early and made muffins from scratch. I milked the chickens and then rode a cow along the fence line on the back forty. Then I brewed some of the coffee you sent."

"Wait a second. You didn't fucking make muffins."

"Okay, I bought muffins. But I warmed them in the oven."

"That's something."

"Then Trisha went off to work and I sat in the window seat reading a Vonnegut novel from before he went goofy, and by the time I looked up it was lunch hour, and I bicycled into town and had a plowman's plate at the pub, and a beautiful Guinness. Some of the workmen were there—I have no idea what they actually work on, but they're dressed in overalls with big boots and such. It's very convincing, even if they just sit in the pub all day. Maybe that *is* their work. Turns out one of 'em is a fan of Trisha's band—of Gorsey Park—so he invited me over to sit with them. I didn't understand much of what they said, but I think we had a grand time, laughing and slapping each other's backs, and the like.

"They wanted to know about basketball. There's a court at the high school and some of them have been playing on Tuesday nights, mainly just to work up a sweat so they feel better about coming to the pub, but still. They asked me to join them. You know what's weird?"

Phillip recognized there was no way to prepare himself for whatever might be coming next. "Go on," he said.

"There seem to be no class distinctions here a'tall. They must know that I don't work for a living . . . but they seem no less kind to me. I don't feel resented—even though I'm a rich outsider, at least by their standards. I'm the jackanapes who married the prettiest girl in town. I'm the idle rich guy that everyone's supposed to hate, regardless of what a jackanapes might actually be. It's just fun to say it out loud. But it worries me."

"What?" Phillip asked.

"That they're so nice. Why are they so fecking nice, Phillip?"

"It's because they're not from New York."

"This place might be growing on me," Spencer said. "Maybe that's the big fucking secret: that people are nice. I would never have seen that coming. Hey, I also wanted to ask you one more thing . . ."

Phillip steeled himself. "What's that?"

"Does this seem like a good idea: I'm thinking of bringing in the sheikhs. I thought it might give us another reason for rejoicing . . ."

Chapter Fifteen

Blue. Sperm.

"Well, there's been a bit of a kerfuffle here," Spencer said to open their next Zoom call.

Phillip knew that his brother might describe Chernobyl as "a kerfuffle." As on every call since their separation, Spencer was showing off another new Zoom background—this one of the Starship Enterprise, except all the stations were manned by cats.

"Go on," Phillip said, for possibly the ten millionth time since his brother's birth.

Spencer described a dinner he and Trisha had attended at her parents' house. Padraig was there, as was one of the other brothers—Peter—who was visiting from Amsterdam.

Phillip noted that these were, in fact, his own brothers, as well.

As Spencer described it, they were all sipping from glasses of Red Breast that had spent some time in port casks, feet up on the ottoman, sleepy-full of beef roast.

Then Patrick leaned forward in his reclining chair—which he referred to as a "declining" chair because they were for old men—and said, "Well, I've something to tell you. And you might not like it."

Trisha had been waiting for this for years. Cancer, she knew.

Patrick went on. "Now that all this DNA business has mostly settled itself and we've gotten used to who's who, what with Phillip turning out to be my boy and Trisha marrying Spencer, I thought it time for me to come clean about something as well."

Lorna looked deep into her whiskey as if there might be a fish in there. The children looked around at one another with dread. Was it an affair he'd confess? That he was a Kazakhstani spy? That he preferred Drogheda United to the Sligo Rovers?

"Out with it, Da," Padraig said. "How much worse can it be than to learn we've Americans in the family?"

"My mother . . ." Patrick said. "I could swear I told you this when you were little but your ma says no."

"Told us what?" Trisha said, waving her hand in the universal signal for 'move along.'"

"She was English," Patrick said, smiling shyly so that they couldn't tell if he was making a joke.

"She was most certainly fucking *not*," Trisha said, sitting forward and setting her whiskey on the floor.

Padraig said, "We've seen where she grew up in County Wicklow, Da. We know what she sounded like. She was no more English than a shillelagh."

"Aye, she grew up here," Patrick said. "But she was born in England. Her parents were English. If you're all about this DNA business then you'd have to consider her English."

Phillip thought: nobody is really entirely who we thought they were—or even who *they* thought they were—any more.

The fire crackled in the hearth, making them jump.

"Oh fer feck's sake, Da," Peter said then. "And I suppose Grandad was Punjabi."

As Spencer described the scene to his brother, Phillip grew quiet on the other end of the call. Spencer could see Phillip biting his lip and leaning in toward the camera, looking as if he'd lost a contact lens and was searching for it on his screen.

"Oh, this is fucking pairfect," Phillip eventually said. "I was just starting to feel maybe the slightest bit Irish after being a Jew my whole life, and now you're telling me that half of me is supposed to hate the other half of me? Who the fuck am I, really? I have no idea."

"Well, actually, it's only twenty-five percent hating another twenty-five percent if the numbers from your DNA test are accurate. But you don't always have to make everything about you."

———

The family convened to talk about what this meant, with everyone having strong feelings that could only work themselves out in the evenings, over a dram—which Spencer learned was shorthand for many drams. They went through a lot of Red Breast working it out.

Padraig took the long view, saying that it didn't matter a whit.

Each of them was who they were regardless of whether an ancestor was Irish or English or even God forbid if they came from Wales. It didn't change anything. It wasn't like learning that your father wasn't your father.

Spencer said quietly, meaning for only Trisha to hear him, "I had a friend in college who was from Buffalo, but he looked pretty normal. Other than the hump and the long beard. But I never met anyone who was from whales."

Trisha elbowed him. Padraig, who'd heard him nonetheless, snorted a laugh.

"I never thought it mattered much," Patrick said then. "I'm with Padraig on this one. She was still your grandmam. Her life was the same as whether she'd been born here rather than come over as a wee lass. She lived the life of an Irishwoman."

Trisha disagreed. "All those years we practiced hating them—the English. Is that all to go to waste then? Like we didn't really mean it?" She shot her whiskey and reached for the bottle on the sideboard and poured herself some more. Spencer waved his tumbler but she ignored him.

He eventually grabbed the bottle and poured another two fingers. As if things weren't confusing enough already lately, the whole thing started him thinking about something he and Phillip had been pondering together since their mother died and their long-dead father turned out not to be either's—and especially now that they were living thousands of miles from each other, neither of them in the place they'd so long thought of as home.

Phillip expressed it quite succinctly: "Who *are* we?" he asked his brother. "I mean *really?*"

Part Four

Jack Elliot

CHAPTER SIXTEEN

The Author's Overall Tone In This Passage

ALTHOUGH HE WAS BORN in 1941, toward the end of the pack in a crowded Irish family (with only his brother Patrick to follow), James William Elliot—Jack, from the day he showed up on this earth—was always heir to the throne. Although there wasn't a throne of any kind, and not much else to inherit. But still: he was the favored son, the favorite child. He was the first of the Elliot children born in America following their move from Ireland, and his parents hoped that his birth marked a change of fortune for the family.

Jack's father, James Senior, had fought in WWI and returned home to factory work in Dublin that he was glad to have, and which provided for his growing family until it didn't. His mother Patricia was raised with three sisters on a farm forty minutes from the dark, expanding city. Few knew she'd once been English. The girls were sent to live abroad with Irish relatives of her father's for reasons that never became clear to anyone, including Patricia.

Jack's parents married in 1932 and emigrated to America seven years later, with five children, to follow James Senior's brother; there was work for James in Boston and then in New York, and in New York the job was good enough for James to buy a small house on Long Island, where he worked in the aviation industry leading up to the next war—which he wondered if they might call "the pretty good war," since the title of "great war" was already taken. His irreverence spread through the family like moss-green eyes, as if determined by their DNA, which may have been the case.

When he was three years old Jack inexplicably took to saluting his siblings as they went about wreaking various forms of havoc throughout the house in Rockville Centre. His older brothers Sean and William (Liam) treated any long object like a hurling stick, any round object like a hurling ball (the cat soon learned not to curl up on himself). His older sisters Katherine, Margaret, and Deirdre attended to whatever child needed either attention or a reprimand. Jack always looked them in the eye with the salute, per military protocol, although they had little time for him. He always took off his hat before saluting, if he was wearing one.

The salute became his trademark outside the family, too. One Sunday, when he was just shy of four years old, they were at church at St. Finbar's and Father Joseph was making his rounds after services, his cassock sweeping back and forth along the brick walkway. It was a steel-cold sunny winter day and the parishioners were eager to retreat to their cars, to their Sunday roasts and their radio programs, whereas Father Joseph was keen to engage them further. He could talk a blue streak, as the Elliots well knew—which was saying something for Irish folk to think that. Jack's father had little time for the chatter. He continued bundling the kids in the car as Father Joseph nattered on.

As the priest stood over Jack on the sidewalk the boy covered his eye with one hand as if blocking out the sun. But the sun was behind the elegant stone church, out of sight.

"I believe the boy's saluting me," the priest observed. "Or perhaps he means it for Jesus?" He looked at James and Patricia for encouragement.

"At ease, private," the priest told Jack, and the hand went down. "Looks like this one might be a future soldier of God," the priest said with a sly smile. But he was only half right.

Jack looked up at the flowing robes. The priest had a weak chin and the puffy eyes of a drinker. The boy had begun talking incessantly of late—sometimes to others, sometimes to himself—as if practicing for a career in radio or politics. His siblings were exhausted with it.

"Aren't you out of uniform in that dress, sir?" he asked the priest.

The family inhabited a boisterous Irish-American household with a father who stumbled home from the pub once a week—on his night out with the boys from work—and was always kindly to his children if not focused on their strengths or even necessarily which one was which.

Although the older Elliot boys enjoyed a head start in sports—they traded their hurling sticks for golf clubs and baseball bats—their brother Jack caught up quickly, playing in the Little League all-star games and being chosen first in gym class and in the streets and schoolyards of Rockville Centre when the kids gathered for pick-up games.

He was a modest standout, never gloating, always grateful for a respect he felt he hadn't earned. As he progressed through school he became known as a natural athlete and the reputation became something he felt obligated to live up to, so he became even better at the sports he played: football, basketball, and baseball, the great American triumvirate. When his brother Patrick followed as the last in the sibling birth order, Jack became his coach—in sports and in life, teaching him to shoot free throws as well as how he could avoid dish duty after dinner by feigning interest in some verse from the New Testament so their mother would lose her focus.

Jack was also forever taking apart everything that he could get his hands on—his transistor radio, the toilet, his mother's blender—just for the puzzle of putting it back together again. The Elliots might be two days without their toaster but then it would work better than it ever had—shooting toast high into the air so the kids could catch the slices like pop flies, one in each hand. When Jack was done reassembling it, the transmission in their dad's Buick no longer clanked.

One time, rebuilding their alarm clocks, Jack told his dad, "I lost a bolt somewhere. Maybe it fell into the cold air return, but I'm hesitant to take the HVAC system apart. I don't really know HVAC. I'm pretty sure I can make a new bolt if I can borrow your soldering iron." When he finished the project their alarm clocks rang with a clear new tone that also had a backbeat.

By high school Jack was the kind of athlete that coaches at other schools had heard about, and he attracted college scouts from Hofstra and the state university system. Academically, he was equally proficient at solving quadratic equations as parsing out the themes of love and revenge in *Wuthering Heights*. He scored off the charts on the new SAT and on the Army Navy College Qualifying Test.

But Jack had been focused on military service since elementary school. He didn't crave glory or conflict: for him it was about the honor and discipline that went along with serving his country, especially as the son of an immigrant lucky enough to call America home. Sure, he'd play football for Army if he got accepted to West Point. But when the U.S. crept into the Vietnam War, quietly at first in the late 1950s, he began preparing to join up, figuring there would be plenty of time for college later on. Which was the rare thing Jack miscalculated.

Chapter Seventeen
Four To Five Minutes

In the summer of 1959 Jack was eighteen and working for the Jews (his mother's phrase) at Kellerman's Resort. In the mornings he served omelets and pancakes and toast with the crusts cut off to the Bernstein family, feeling like Vincent Price in *The Invisible Man*: like he could watch them without being noticed.

The mother was an elegant, timeless beauty who carried herself with an insouciance that said: *I don't give a flying fuck*. The older daughter was the opposite, constantly glancing around the room to measure who might be looking at her. She ate with dainty exaggeration, a pinky extended from her orange juice glass as if she were sipping champagne on a yacht.

The other daughter—her smooth, round features framed by dark hair that highlighted the patinaed copper of her eyes—ignored everything, her button nose buried in the Updike she was reading. She poked at a soft-boiled egg with one of those tiny spoons Jack had never seen before this summer—and which made no sense to him: if you're eating, why take so many tiny spoonfuls? Why not just use a larger spoon?

She was a girl everyone would notice, yet she seemed indifferent to the attention, didn't even hear the young man opposite her at the communal table when he tried to amuse her. Kibitzing, he'd heard them call this corny joking—which Jack had thought was one of those communist Jewish enclaves in the recent state of Israel. When he carried their dishes back into the kitchen after breakfast one morning, Jack put his lips to the young girl's coffee cup, trying to match them to the faint color her lipstick had imprinted on the white ceramic.

Later that day he saw her hurrying past the back door of the kitchen; she slowed at the sight of him. Jack knew he was handsome in a particularly Irish way—sandy hair and a light constellation of freckles—and the mothers back home were always introducing their daughters; but here in Jewville he enjoyed his anonymity. Sure, he might woo one of the waitresses in the tavern after the dinner shift, and he'd stolen a few kisses from a big-hipped red-head with a Brooklyn accent, but he was, as always, focused on the task at hand: keep his head down, work hard, put away as much cash as he could for some future that was vague but promising.

When he spoke to Jenny she seemed relieved. She was a rare wild breed caged in this resort full of dull pigeons. He would happily facilitate her escape. But carrying on with the guests was the first thing they were warned against by the aging gangster who oversaw the kitchen. Still, even to a rule-abiding young man like Jack Elliot, some risks were worth taking.

He had no idea whether she'd consider meeting him at the dock that evening as he proposed but he felt like an outlaw suggesting it. There were three weeks left in the summer and he'd proven among the hardest working of the staff—they couldn't afford to be without him at the end of the season, when the soft college boys were returning home early to buy their accounting books and heading back to class. Jack had nothing in front of him, so everything was in front of him.

When he kissed Jenny in the rowboat, with the candle flames gyrating in the bow and stern (his roommate's proven aphrodisiac, or so he claimed), Jack let the kiss linger. He did not press his body forward. Jenny leaned slightly toward him. Her fingers sought his for a firm, gentle squeeze. They both felt a charge run through them, as if the lake had been struck by lightning, as if electricity had rippled across the surface of the water, up the gunwales of the rowboat and into them. Neither would feel such a charge again for the rest of their lives.

They stayed out in the boat until nearly morning—Jack had brought a blanket although it was a hot Catskill night, humid and unrelenting. They spread the blanket across the seat but there was no place in the boat for them to lie beside each other, and so they sat, his arm around her, and then him leaning on one gunnel and her leaning back against him.

When their arms or legs went to sleep Jack rowed them around the lake. Jenny watched his muscles clenching and releasing as he leaned forward with the oars. His biceps danced as he pulled backward to propel the boat.

"This may be the most uncomfortable place for a tryst a boy has ever imagined," Jenny said.

"I hadn't thought past the romantic part," Jack said.

"The candles are a nice touch," Jenny said. "But the seats are a natural form of birth control." She laughed, then grew quiet, and then he grew quiet and she realized he was probably Catholic, and she didn't know any Catholics, and then they both laughed at the silence that came between them. Which dissipated with the laughter.

He *was* a believer in the Church but he also believed in kindness and in doing no harm, so many months later, when they did eventually make love for the first time, he used a condom. It felt right even if the church deemed it a sin.

They met at the dock for the remaining nights that Jenny and her family were at Kellerman's. It wasn't what he'd wanted, but how could he not love this beautiful, vulnerable girl?

In the morning following each of those nights, Phyllis talked about Jerry Rothstein, leaving out only the most intimate details but trying to get Jenny to imagine them. Always back in the room first since Jack had to work the breakfast shift, Jenny never let on that she was also out all night, allowing Phyllis to focus on herself and brag about her own budding romance without ever even conceiving that Jenny—who'd served up Jerry Rothstein to her like a T-bone to a hungry lion—was pursuing a romance of her own.

Chapter Eighteen
El Dio De Los Inocentes

BACK ON LONG ISLAND Jack saw Jenny almost every night; that winter his family hung a Christmas stocking for her above the brick fireplace in their living room in the house in Rockville Centre. It bulged with small gifts they'd bought for the Jewess, as they called her, not unkindly. Jenny was trying to finish high school early and preparing to take classes at Nassau Community College the following fall. Jack was working as a bar manager at night and following a strict workout regimen during the days to prepare for Army basic training.

Jenny dreaded mentioning the stocking to her parents, but when she did, her mother said, "That's good. Jews never have anywhere to go on Christmas." But Jenny knew what she meant was: thank God Jenny was focusing on something other than her dead brother and ancient Egyptian curses.

Jenny had mentioned Noah to Jack on that hot Catskill night when they'd begun courting. When he drove to Hewlett to watch her cheerleading during her senior year he recognized the depth of her loss.

"You don't really seem the cheerleading type," he said one day as they were drinking hot cocoa back at the Bernstein house after a football game. She'd changed out of her uniform in the car as soon as the game ended. Jack marveled at how girls could change clothes without ever really taking them off.

"It's a disguise," Jenny whispered.

"Who—or what—are you hiding from?" Jack asked.

Jenny looked around to make sure her mother wasn't lurking.

"You've seen little girls dressed up like cheerleaders for Halloween, haven't you? As a cheerleader I can scream like an imbecile for a bunch of football players without anybody knowing what I'm really screaming about. They can't accuse me of being depressed when my main hobby is to yell passionately about adolescent boys scoring touchbacks."

"Touchdowns," he said.

She looked at him intensely—a look that was half smile, half snarl, revealing her perfect mah-jongg tile teeth. "I can think about my brother all I want when I'm wearing the stupid poodle skirt and waving pom-poms like a fucking retard."

"I had no idea," Jack said.

"It's classic misdirection," Jenny said. Misdirection was the key to the Mr. Wizard trick that her brother had taught her. Jenny would hone and reuse this skill for the rest of her life—not just because it came in handy, but because possibly it was keeping Noah alive in the afterlife. At the very least, it kept him that way for Jenny, who became a wizard at misdirection.

"The disguise even fooled my psychiatrist, who's as dumb as the line breakers on the team," Jenny said then.

"Linebackers," Jack corrected. "You're seeing a psychiatrist?"

"Yes. My parents insisted. Because I'm sad. Apparently you're not supposed to be sad when your favorite person on the whole planet dies horribly and it's your fault." She flashed back to Noah's broken body on the pavement of the Garden State Parkway. How she thought at first that he was faking the way his limbs bent at impossible angles—another one of his jokes.

"Aren't your parents sad, too?"

"It's easier for them to be worried about me. It's a simpler emotion to muster."

"Is that what the psychiatrist said?"

"I don't need a psychiatrist to know that," Jenny said. "I don't really need a psychiatrist at all, except it's proven convenient in getting my parents off my back insisting I be more cheerful."

"Why are they on your back?"

"Because they think I'm too sad! Which I am—unbelievably, unbearably, heartbreakingly sad."

"I'm so sorry," Jack said, because he was, and because he had no idea what else to say. He pushed the marshmallow in his hot chocolate around with one finger. "It wasn't your fault, despite what you say. It was a horrible accident. But I see why you might think that," Jack said.

"I'll always think it," Jenny said. "But maybe one day I'll stop believing it. I want to show you something," Jenny said.

Jack looked nervous. In his limited experience, that's what somebody said before revealing something you didn't want to see.

"It's not what you're thinking," she said.

"How do you know what I'm thinking? Maybe I'm thinking about the role of women in Hemingway. Maybe I'm considering which ratchet set to buy."

"You're thinking about sex," Jenny said.

He sat forward in the red kitchen chair. "I'm afraid that you're going to give it up to me—your virginity—because your brother is dead. And because I'm sympathetic. That you're going to mix the two things up somehow."

"That's a weird thing to say," Jenny said. "Sweet, but weird. But just keep in mind; we're alive, and I want to live as fully as I possibly can. For both of us."

Jack wasn't sure if by "both of us" she meant her and him or her and her brother.

"But that's not what I was going to show you," Jenny said. She flashed a cryptic smile. She ran up to her bedroom and came back with a deck of crisp Bicycle playing cards. She shuffled the cards with the casual confidence of a blackjack dealer.

"Pick a card," she told Jack, fanning out the deck.

He looked at her closely but her eyes remained on the cards. She wasn't giving anything away.

He slid a card from the half-moon they made in her small hand.

"Now show it to me," Jenny said.

"You want me to show you the card? How does that make any sense?" But he held up the three of diamonds for her to see.

She went to the telephone and dialed a number. Her fingernails clicked in the slots in the rotary phone.

"Mr. Wizard, please," she said a moment later. "Yes, I'll hold." Then after another short pause she said, "Hello, Mr. Wizard. Please tell Jack his card."

The deep, tired, gravelly voice on the other end—it sounded vaguely African-American to Jack—told him his card. Jenny took the receiver back and hung up the phone. And then she cried. Her body shook and tears fell on her argyle sweater and Jack, not knowing what to do, put his arms around her and held her.

Eventually she wiped her eyes on the backs of her wrists and sat up straight. She put the cards down on the bright, mottled yellow linoleum of the table. "That was my brother's trick. Noah's trick. Now he's gone and I have to be Mr. Wizard, misdirecting my parents with this whole cheerleader chazzerai. It's what will keep Noah alive. The ancient Egyptians taught me that much." She thought about the false doors in Egyptian tombs, meant to link the dead back to the living. That was a form of misdirection, too.

"I'm sorry—cheerleading what?" Jack said.

"Chazzerai. It's a Yiddish word. It means junk, or craziness. Or bullshit, really. You have to promise never to tell my parents that I was crying. They'll have me carted off to Bellevue. Or—even worse—Wellesley."

Jack took her hands, felt the warmth of them. He imagined them kneading the muscles in his neck because that's all he allowed himself to imagine. "I won't tell anyone," he said. "But one day, when you're my wife, you'll be required to show me how that trick works."

Chapter Nineteen
H21-C

Jenny Bernstein and Jack Elliot were married at the Nassau County Courthouse in Hempstead in early 1961, with Jack's younger brother Patrick as the best man and Jenny's sister Phyllis as a recalcitrant maid of honor. Phyllis wore a low-cut black dress but Jenny, wearing a tight sculpture of white lace, managed to render her sister invisible.

The civil ceremony allowed the couple to avoid the competing rituals of the Jews and Irishmen who might have held strong views on their union. Afterward, they went for an Italian dinner in lower Manhattan that Jerry Rothstein, Phyllis's beau, made a great show of paying for. They drank Chianti, and then tiny glasses of amaro with the cannoli. It felt simultaneously exotic and underwhelming, but the newlyweds only cared about being married. They'd have been content to eat toasted cheese sandwiches at home and hurry to the bedroom sooner.

Jenny loved Jack without question or reservation—he was kind, handsome, ambitious, well read, and emotionally strong. The marriage gave her the opportunity to get out of her parents' house, which was key to her getting over Noah's death. She was aware that change was supplanting permanence, as the Egyptians might have seen it. And that living in a new place—even one that was only three miles from her parents' house—was crucial to her recovery.

Jack's love for Jenny wasn't what he'd expected, or hoped for. It might prove a barrier to his plans. But she'd stormed his heart like a Viking—fierce, fast, relentless. He abdicated to it, and strove to weave it into the narrative he was creating for his future and what he hoped to accomplish.

Jack enlisted in the US Army that winter. He began his training at Mitchel Field, a short drive from the brick apartment he and Jenny rented in Hewlett, not far from the high school that she cringed at every time she drove past. Jack sometimes dropped her off at Nassau Community in Garden City if she had an early class (she was planning to study literature, or maybe anthropology, the apartment was already filling with her books), until his schedule became more erratic—something he said he could not explain to her. He was also training secretly further out on Long Island, she discovered when she found train tickets to Montauk in his jacket pocket. On those days he'd come home "knackered," as he put it, barely able to stay awake long enough after dinner to help plan their honeymoon—to Quebec, the most European of North American cities, Jenny had read. Sometimes he had grease on his hands that wouldn't come off in the shower, even using the Lava soap.

One evening Jack returned home late, with flowers and a bottle of Asti Spumante—which Jenny knew he thought of as exotic, although she remembered it from high school football victory parties. Still she was charmed, trying to figure out what they were celebrating. She put the flowers in a milk bottle and set them on the Irish wake table that had been a gift from Jack's family.

"What's the occasion?" Jenny asked. She was wearing one of his white dress shirts over a pair of plaid slacks, the sleeves carefully folded back up all the way to her biceps. Jack could see the faint outline of the black lace bra she'd debuted shortly after the wedding. Jenny said she had a drawer full of surprises for him that she'd reveal over time if he was good.

Jack winced at the question. They'd both known this was coming.

"Where to?" Jenny asked.

"Saigon. It's a city in Vietnam. In Southeast Asia."

"I know where Vietnam is," Jenny said. "We get the Newsday."

"We're going over to help the South Vietnamese. As advisors. It's an administrative mission."

Jenny considered whether he was naïve or protecting her. "Helicopters seem like awkward places to administrate from," she said. "But what do I know. I'm just a Long Island housewife. Who probably isn't going to be visiting Quebec any time soon. Or shopping the maternity section at Korvettes."

"It's my first assignment," Jack said. "There'll be more choices later on. These people need our help."

She knew Jack couldn't not help people in pain—which had drawn he and Jenny together in the first place. But which made the military a poor choice for him, since the world was a rollicking shitstorm filled with pain.

"What about those of us who need you here?" Jenny said, and then she left the room because she knew it was an argument that couldn't be won. She came back into the kitchen and opened the fizzy alcohol with a cork-pop that put a final exclamation point on their conversation. At least they could get started on the baby, she thought. Which they worked at later that evening.

———————

He was gone by spring and Jenny never saw him again. He hadn't owned many clothes in the first place so the closets barely seemed emptier without the few pairs of khakis and half a dozen button-down shirts. Jenny noticed that the Jameson seemed to disappear just as quickly without him.

At first she received two or three letters from him each week, with a funny anecdote about a meal he couldn't identify or a description of a soldier he'd met who was from Wyoming. When his correspondence slowed she recognized it wasn't possible to sustain that pace of letters that said so little. She sensed a stoic distress behind the words, and then behind the lack of them.

In one letter home Jack hinted at how Vietnam had changed him. "Despite some of the terrible things I've seen here, living in a different place reveals things to you. Sometimes wonderful things, as your hero Howard Carter might have said. We should live someplace else for a while when we get the chance."

Jenny was relieved that his letters in no way resembled those of Lady Duff Gordon's—not in length, certainly not in level of detail, and Jack wouldn't allow himself to die in a foreign land without seeing his true love again. Would he?

In response, Jenny sent him the silver ring with the colored stone in it that Noah had buried in the "yard of back." It had stopped fitting over even her pinkie.

"Wear this around your neck, with your dog tags, and think of me," she wrote. "You can bring it home and give it back to me before we run off to live abroad. What do you think about Vienna? My people came from there and I'd very much like to see it."

By the time Jack's helicopter went down in the jungle outside of Bien Hoa Jenny had let go of hopes or aspirations for their future because they were too difficult to nurture in the cold brick apartment thousands of miles from her husband. She hadn't seen Jack in what seemed like almost as long as she'd known him. He went down shortly before Jenny gave birth to Phillip; the army wouldn't even report him missing until a year later. Everyone wondered who the father might be, although Jenny insisted it was Jack despite the impossibility—it was a way of keeping her husband alive. Jenny couldn't help but wonder if Noah's ring had been a comfort to him or somehow led to his demise.

Above the thick foreign jungle, when something wracked the back of his helicopter, Jack's first thoughts were for the Vietnamese soldiers in his charge. He wondered how he'd safely extricate them from the rough terrain. His last thoughts were for his younger brother Patrick, and for his one true love, who would live another five decades without ever finding another man to replace or replicate how he'd impacted her own still-pumping heart.

Part Five

Phillip and Spencer

CHAPTER TWENTY
1428 SE 19ᵗʰ Ave.

PHILLIP'S FAVORITE PART OF any new real estate project was walking through a building when demolition was half done. It was like one of those drawings that showed time in layers, where the same landscape was filled simultaneously with dinosaurs and skyscrapers.

That was when unforeseen discoveries were made. In one old house in Westchester many years ago Phillip's crew disinterred three sets of oak pocket doors with beautifully wrought cast-iron face plates buried beneath sheetrock. In a Brooklyn multiplex they'd found a mason jar full of silver half dollars from the 1920s. In a Manhattan townhouse, neat stacks of Victorian pornography appeared as they claw-hammered down the original lathe and plaster walls. Phillip knew that houses had histories and personalities in the same way that people did—and buildings were more interesting and exhibited far better character.

Or you found nothing—or the plumber or the electrician ran off with the gold bars or Graf Zeppelin stamps or the Honus Wagner baseball cards—but you could still enjoy the satisfaction of stripping out defunct systems like knob-and-tube wiring or rusty cast iron pipes and reinvigorating an ailing structure for another century of life.

Phillip and Marty often walked over to the eight-plex job site in their neighborhood in Southeast Portland in the late afternoons, when the crews took off their hard hats and respirators and got ready to leave for the day. The couple would point out their favorite architectural details in houses along the way—an elegant eyebrow dormer hidden on the side of a roof, or a set of wooden pilasters topped with Doric details on a Greek Revival. Often they'd make a longer loop walk through Laurelhurst Park and Lone Fir Cemetery.

Strolling through the graveyard Phillip had taken to offering greetings to his favorite residents, who were becoming as familiar to him as the few friends they'd made in Portland so far.

"Hello, George Strowbridge, born in 1866," or "Good afternoon Anna Winters, a lot's happened since you arrived here," he might say.

Marty, holding his hand might reply, "Honey, speak up. They're a hundred and fifty years old."

Phillip liked to visit Paul C. Lind, whose headstone was decorated with a Scrabble board made of stone tiles. "I hope you got that triple word score for 'deceased,'" Phillip might say. He made note that some of Lone Fir's residents had left their names on streets throughout the city—obvious examples of legacy in action.

After visiting the job site and assessing progress, they'd often head to Three Doors Down, off Hawthorne, where'd they'd sip Prosecco on tap and eat pasta almost as good as something you could get on the Lower East Side of Manhattan. If Phillip was feeling expansive he and Marty might wander across the street to Greater Trumps—named for a nineteenth century British novel, not the disgraced former president—one of the city's remaining, grandfathered cigar bars, and Phillip might puff a Davidoff Primeros Nicaraguan Maduro. He'd drink a Jameson in honor of his newly found heritage and talk to Marty about his brother, whom he missed. Even the parts that made you want to garrote him. Marty might take the cigar from his mouth and puff on it like a teamster in an old movie, blowing a plume of smoke before handing it back to him.

On one site visit, when Phillip brought a case of beer for the crew to share once they were off the clock, the general contractor—Anatoli—handed him a dirty envelope, creased in many places and half covered in plaster dust. Anatoli was a hard worker—a Russian boss who wasn't afraid to swing a hammer alongside his team.

"We found tucked beside doorframe of upstairs bedroom when we pull down plaster," Anatoli explained. He held his hands up in a kind of defense—the international posture of general contractors.

"What is it?" Phillip asked.

"Is letter, maybe? I don't know." Anatoli turned away, as if to check on an empty plumbing fixture box. Phillip also knew that for contractors, anything outside their purview could only be trouble.

"From the city?"

"Also this I don't know," Anatoli said.

Phillip put the envelope inside his jacket pocket.

An hour later, as dusk settled over Portland and an alarming number of crows circled overhead or settled in the trees, Phillip sat on the front steps of the renovated, furnished foursquare he and Marty were renting. He opened a Fresh Squeezed citrusy IPA from Deschutes Brewery—a beer he was becoming enamored of—and took a letter out of the envelope. It read:

Portland, Ore.
March 1857

Dear Jackson:

Arrived Ore after arduous long journey along the trail. Uncle Jumpy is well and we have joined him in the house on the east side of the Willamet. Will work in the orchards with him, there is much to be done. I'm sorry to say we lost Albert to the Collera in Neb. Terr. He was a fine boy and will be missed. Life will be very different going forward, I think.

Despite our talk, will not be coming back east again.

God Bless, your loving Mary.

Phillip's first response was sadness, like when you receive bad news over the phone. Then he wondered: is this a sign? But of what? He also thought: everyone is displaced. Everyone is from somewhere else.

Then he imagined the rough trip across the continent in, probably, a covered wagon? What circumstance might drive someone to take that risk? He nearly wept over the end of the relationship and the fine, dead boy.

And then he thought: perhaps Mary was escaping a worse fate. Maybe Jackson was a shitheel, a deadbeat, a bully and a drunk. And was she even his wife? And who was Albert? Their son? A younger brother to them both? And Uncle Jumpy?

Marty came out onto the porch, splashing Eyrie Vineyards pinot noir on the old pine boards, surprised to find Phillip tearful. He read her the letter. She cut right to the heart of the mystery, something Phillip didn't even see.

"If Mary was writing to someone back east, why was the letter stuck in a doorframe in a house in Portland?"

"You're right, how did I not see that?" Phillip said. "I'm liable to lose my private investigator's license. Also there's no stamp on the envelope even though it has this address."

"Did Jackson follow Mary and bring the letter with him?" Marty asked. "Did she never send it? And if she didn't send it, did Jackson even know she'd made it west? Did he ever hear from her again?"

"Or maybe Mary died before she could send it and old, creepy Uncle Jumpy found the letter and stuck it in the doorframe because he didn't know what else to do with it."

Marty set her wine glass on the wooden porch railing.

"It's so *tactile*. I mean it's history unfurling before our eyes. The history of actual, particular people."

"It is," Philip agreed.

She looked down at him with a sad smile. She sipped pinot with her beautiful lips.

"What else?" Phillip asked.

"Well, we've just taken our own trail west. And we don't know if we'll be going back east again, either."

"Ah," Phillip said.

When Phillip told Spencer about the letter his brother said, "Wow. Uncle Jumpy. That sounds creepy. I wonder what happened to them all."

"I'm going to find out," Phillip said. He was already considering the first steps of an investigation.

"Wait, what? Why on earth would you follow up on this? Why don't you just frame the letter and hang it in the lobby? Or give it to the historical society?"

They already both knew the answer.

"Mom," Phillip said.

"Okay, hold on a second, Hercule Marple. Are you suggesting that Mom sent you on a quest into the wild lands of Portland, Oregon, to find this letter? Like, her message was about something *specific* you were meant to find, and you think it's a letter that's been buried *inside the walls* of an old building in a city none of us have really even been to before, and that by discovering something about this random letter accidentally uncovered by some Russian mobster contractor you're going to receive, what, life instructions, or a secret treasure map leading to a cache of hundred-year-old Mars bars?"

"Mom did say things would be revealed," Phillip said. "We never talked about whether we thought she had something particular in mind for us to find—this letter, for example—or something more generic, like that we'd discover a new passion in our travels. Mountain climbing, or Irish dancing, I don't know. Or maybe she just knew that *something* would happen, whether specific or generic. Or maybe she knew that we'd find something specific even if she didn't know what it might be."

"Or do we find something—or *think* we have—just because we start looking?" Spencer asked.

"I'm trying to avoid the mystical in all this and attribute it to coincidence, but this letter is all about somebody going to live somewhere else. And being changed by it. It's not that far fetched. It's hard to see this as entirely random, especially given that Mom's other quest for us led us to our fathers. So she's got some credibility. Which makes it all worse."

"It's even more confounding because she was out of her gourd toward the end," Spencer pointed out. "It may be synchronicity or some shite like that. Or we may be following the random instructions of a total nutter."

"Which still doesn't mean something won't be revealed to us."

"Yep. There's that, too," Spencer admitted.

Chapter Twenty-One
Rook and King

In Ballydraiocht, since the band had politely spurned his offer to garner new gigs for them, Spencer took to playing at open mic nights at other pubs around the county. He made a few Irish friends, which Trisha was happy for. And while his brother continued to build forward momentum toward, well, Spencer wasn't sure toward what, in Portland, Spencer searched for his own mystery—whether he thought he'd find one or not.

He vowed to visit a castle of some kind every week—whether a castle converted to a bakery or brewpub, or a tourist castle, or a pile-of-stones castle hidden just behind a graveyard in some town so small it didn't have a name sign on the outskirts. He suspected castles might have secrets to reveal through bloodstained stone or caches of Roman gold or some shite like that. He called it his quest, though he knew it wasn't. But maybe he could fake his way to some kind of revelation. He devised this strategy in reference to his vague understanding of his mother's Egyptian period, as if his exploration of castles could somehow extend her legacy of searching.

Phillip's Uncle Jumpy letter got Spencer to thinking: what were they both looking for, anyway? What could possibly be revealed to them, especially following the revelations about their fathers, which—to their mom's credit—she had kicked off with a few cryptic words? Wasn't that enough discovery for a lifetime? Couldn't they just retire from investigative work and concentrate on drinking and forgetting, like every detective on every mystery show he'd ever watched? For another thing, castles were notorious for being drafty.

He brought this up to Trisha one night as they were eating an Irish stew that Spencer had made in the slow cooker. It wasn't bad for his first attempt, although he drank as much stout during preparation as went into the dish. The Peat Bog Faeries were streaming through the Bose speakers in the background, the distant bagpipes an atmospheric touch.

"I've no idea what you're looking for, either. But I still hope you find it. But it's still okay if you don't. I don't know what to say: I'm not driven like that."

Spencer high-graded a couple more carrots out of the stew—they were deliciously caramelized. "Maybe it's just curiosity. Maybe it was ingrained in us by our wacky mom, who could make a cold case out of misplacing the laundry soap."

"Yeah. Your brother's got it too," Trisha observed.

"Yes. He makes me look almost like a reasonable person. You should have seen the situation room he set up when he was first trying to find out who our father was, when we thought it was going to turn out to be the same father."

"It's like an addiction," Trisha said. "You can't help yourself: when something comes up, instead of reaching for the whiskey like normal folk you get on the Googles and start researching the names of actors from obscure black and white films or what flying dinosaurs were called. But maybe the father thing was your only true quest and the rest of this is a result of your mother's dementia."

"Pterosaurs," Spencer said. "But they weren't actually dinosaurs. They were flying reptiles."

"Yeah, like that," Trisha said.

———

At the first castle he visited, Blarney, Spencer was purely a tourist. And when Spencer was a tourist at a museum or castle or the world's largest dog chew toy, he felt obligated to read every interpretive sign, every guidebook entry. Trisha accompanied him on the trip but skipped the castle tour. She read a sizeable chunk of Keith Richards's autobiography in one of the many gardens—actually in several of the many gardens, since Spencer was gone for so long in the castle and she wanted to stay in the sun as it moved across the sky. She ate lunch in the Stable Yard Café. Later, she went back for a coffee.

When Spencer met her there on her second visit she said, "You're not likely to buy the place. Did you have to inspect the plumbing and the foundation and all?"

Spencer gave her that disarming smile that could win over a Buckingham Palace guard. He sat across from her and consulted his visitor's map, making sure he hadn't inadvertently skipped a room or outbuilding. He ordered a cappuccino, and made fun of the tiny spoon. But he was glad for the tiny chocolate biscuit—what he previously would have called a cookie—crowded onto the saucer.

"How was it?" she said. "You've been gone for days." She sipped her own cappuccino, milk foam gathering above her upper lip in a way that was even more adorable since she was unaware of it. Spencer thought: that's what she'll look like if she gets old and grows a moustache.

"My favorite part was the poison garden. Except for a couple of screaming kids. So I told them that the mandrake tasted just like hot cocoa."

"You didn't."

"No, I didn't. I told them that the ricin tasted like taffy."

On his regular Zoom call with Phillip that week Spencer told him about the Barney Castle visit.

"I think you mean Blarney Castle. Where the famous stone is?" Phillip asked.

"Named for the big retarded purple dinosaur?"

"I don't think so. Aren't you supposed to kiss the stone for good luck?"

"Not luck. They say if you kiss it you'll never be at a loss for words."

"You must have Frenched it."

"You can rest easy, brother. I didn't kiss it. It was covered with lipstick and drool. They want you to lean over backwards—I think so it's easier to slit your throat. They actually have a professional hand-holder, which I didn't even know was a career. "

"Any secrets revealed to you? Revelations? Whispered voices with information to set you on a path?"

"Nada. Nunca. Bubkis," Spencer said.

A week later Spencer drove by himself to his next castle—Ballygantry—in some places barely more than a few piles of loosely organized stones. He was alone on the site overlooking the Irish Sea. He smoked a short Nub cigar with a thick ring gauge and a Connecticut wrapper as he sat on the front steps of what might have been the main entrance to the home ten centuries ago, imagining himself as Laird.

Spencer wandered the castle grounds, sitting on rock walls, standing inside airy, roofless rooms that hosted swallows nests, thinking: *they've really let the place go.* He walked out into the grassy expanses beyond the ruins and listened to sheep in distant fields, waiting like the Buddha for enlightenment, like Newton for an apple to fall on his head. Something. Anything. He wished that Phillip was there with him. They'd never been this far apart, for this long, in their lives. He discovered that he missed his brother, but that wasn't exactly a secret.

Not long after Ballygantry, Spencer and Trisha drove to Dublin and stayed at the same hotel where he and Phillip had stayed on their first visit to Ireland, when they discovered that Patrick Elliot was Phillip's father. They ate Indian food that rivaled places in New York's Alphabet City. On Saturday they took the tour of Dublin Castle. Since Trisha had contacts in the tourism industry they were able to get a private showing early in the morning, before the buses arrived.

As Spencer told Phillip in their next Zoom call, "Much to my surprise I'm obsessed with the whole castle thing. I don't know what it is."

"It's usually an old stone building where rich people lived," Phillip said.

"It's not the castles themselves but everything surrounding them. I'd like to know what they were so afraid of, building all those turrets," Spencer said. "I mean marauders, sure. And rapists. And yes, pillagers, Vikings, Dragons. Probably the English, too—maybe they were afraid the English would break into the kitchens and start cooking." After a moment's pause he added, "I have a theory."

"Go on then," Phillip said.

"Okay, two theories. It's the stuff Mom taught us. The puzzles and mysteries. Like when she was crazy for the Egyptians as a child. And all the treasure hunts and scavenger hunts she set up for us. We just can't let go of unanswered questions. We have to uncover the solution to every conundrum we're confronted with."

"So we learned that obsessiveness from Mom. I actually have my own theory about that," Phillip said.

"Sure, let's interrupt my theories to hear your theory."

"It's like this . . . the little mysteries are a metaphor for The Big Mystery . . ."

"You mean the one about why I'm so handsome?"

"Death, my brother. Since we don't have any way of knowing where we go or what happens to us when we're dead, we solve these little mysteries—Easter Island, ghosts, the lateral thinking puzzles Mom gave us—because we're really trying to learn the secret to the Big Mystery."

"Okay . . . maybe . . ."

"But wait! There's more!"

"So you're going to interrupt my theory with *two* theories?"

"The reason people want to see new places is to prepare them for the Big Vacation—the final one: death. The afterlife, if there is one. It's why people travel and relocate. I think it was what Mom was trying to communicate to us, but figured we'd be better off learning it directly for ourselves. Hence the order to move away from home."

"Your theories have something in common," Spencer said. "They're morbid. Are you done, or do you want to interrupt me even further?"

"No. That is all."

"Then back to my second theory," Spencer said. "I think the need to solve mysteries was passed down to us genetically. Like there's a DNA sequence and Mom had it and she passed it on to us. We can't help ourselves."

"Either way, shouldn't we have moved beyond it all by now?" Phillip asked. "Especially given the recent paternal revelations? Do we really need to solve any more mysteries? People overcome upbringing *and* genetic predisposition all the time. Just because you have a gene variation that predicts baldness doesn't mean you're absolutely one hundred percent going to be a cue ball in later life."

"Yes, exactly. It's like Trisha says: I'm a grown man and maybe I should have evolved past some of this childhood stuff, or rejiggered the genetic factory settings with plain good sense. She said it nicely, in a wifely way, so that it wasn't like criticism. But that can't be right—the part about me being a grown man."

"I have one more theory," Phillip said. "A new one. We already rehashed that whole nature vs. nurture debate. And I really don't want this to be like *Groundhog Day*."

"Or *Run, Lola, Run*. Or *50 First Dates*, or *Primer*, or *Source Code*, or any of the other derivative movies with the same exact story line. It's kind of funny when you think about it: that they keep making movies over and over again about a day that repeats over and over again. But I see what you're getting at. What's your new theory?" Spencer asked.

"Well, possibly it's not so much who or what or why, but *where* . . . Sure DNA and upbringing make us who we are. That ground has been covered. A lot. But so does place—place also makes us who we are. So maybe it's not even so much where we're *going*—now or after death—as where we're *from*. Or maybe it's both, I don't know. You and I, maybe we're New Yorkers no matter where we go. There'll always be Orange Julius running through our veins, even if we move."

"Or Gray's Papaya," Spencer added.

"Or Gray's Papaya."

"But not Papaya King. Or Papaya Dog."

"Obviously," Phillip said.

"I'd also make the case that the Broadway and 72nd location was always better than the Sixth Avenue or Eighth Avenue locations. Which explains why those went out of business. But back to your theory. I need to think about that. Especially now that we're both in new places. So it's PNA, rather than DNA. The 'P' being place. So the whole moving thing was Mom's ruse to help us discover that we were already home!"

"That doesn't really make any sense," Phillip said. "But I like it."

Chapter Twenty-Two

Dover

THE BOYS' FIRST EXTENDED trip away from home as kids was a week-long visit to their grandparents in Florida when Phillip was six and Spencer was five. Aunt Phyllis told Jenny she was insane to take the two young monsters on an airplane, but Jenny knew that she could distract them long enough to get through the flight. And she could always put a little Nyquil in their Cokes as necessary.

Somewhere above Delaware they began to get fidgety. Phillip was thinking too much, and that was never good. Spencer was trying to eat his seat cushion.

"Don't we have any other grandparents we could visit?" Phillip asked. "My friends all have a lot of grandparents."

"I'm sorry, sweetie. Your other grandparents died a long time ago. Spencer, don't chew on that, it's dirty."

"What about other aunts and uncles? And cousins?" Phillip asked as his brother lowered his tray table and began licking it.

Jenny pushed the tray table back upright and rifled through her bag for a bagel. "Here, eat this," she said to Spencer. Then to Phillip she said, "You have Aunt Phyllis and Uncle Jerry. And cousin Leah."

"Yeah, but aren't there any more? Mark Levitt has like ten grand-parents. And hundreds of cousins."

"Mark Levitt's mother married four times. Your dad was an only child, and his parents died when he was still young. And then he died young."

"Isn't there anybody else?"

Jenny looked over at Spencer, who had fallen asleep with the bagel still in his mouth. "Nope. Sorry. All dead," Jenny said. Then she pulled out a coloring book and the small box of Crayolas for Phillip. This wasn't a conversation she wanted to have with her children, especially since she was outright lying to them—which she chose to see more simply as misdirection.

The airplane trip and the vacation in general were disorienting for Phillip, although Spencer adapted right away. Phillip was uncomfortable with how sunny and warm it was in Florida in the middle of winter. He kept asking what was wrong, as if he'd finally gotten this whole season thing figured out, and now: this. He constantly squinted at the sky as if to reprimand the sun for being so bright in February.

When they arrived at Jenny's parents' place on Collins Avenue in Miami, Spencer ran toward the ocean out behind the apartment while Jenny was unloading their suitcases from the rental car—just like he did back home when they went to Atlantic Beach. He seemed shocked at first to see the water there, then just accepted it with delight while Phillip stood ruminating. When Phillip's expression turned serious he looked just like Jack, Jenny thought—then she reminded herself that he actually looked just like Patrick, his real father, who looked a lot like Jack.

Jenny sprinted after Spencer as he splashed into the shallow water with his sneakers still on.

"We NEVER go in the ocean without Mommy," she told him. But as soon as she let go of his arm he was pulling off his Keds and jumping with both feet into the pockets of foam puddling in the wet sand.

"Spencer," Jenny said, her tone sharp enough to catch his attention.

Phillip watched from the softer white sand that burned his feet. Jenny could tell he was trying to figure things out, to understand how a completely different environment could exist here, just an airplane ride away from the snow that had piled up around their house on Long Island. She could practically see his little brain firing new pathways, taking in the stimuli and processing it.

Phillip didn't sleep well the whole week they were in Florida. One night he climbed out of the fold out bed in the living room that he was sharing with Spencer and wandered into the kitchen, where a light still shone.

His grandfather was sitting at the table reading a book about Israel.

"I can't sleep, Papa," Phillip said, rubbing his eyes with his fists. He expected his grandfather to comfort him, to lead him back to bed and tuck him in.

"I cannot sleep, either," Samuel said. "When your mother couldn't sleep as a little girl we used to drive her around the neighborhood in the back of our old Buick." Samuel patted his lap for Phillip to climb up.

"Are you a good driver, Papa?" Phillip asked.

"Not according to your grandmother, but I haven't run anyone over yet."

"Have you always lived in Florida?" Phillip asked.

"Once I lived far away in Austria. Across the ocean! And we lived in Brooklyn. That's where your mother grew up. Then we lived in a house in Hewlett, not far from where you live now."

"Do you have any pictures?"

"I do have pictures, yes," Samuel said. He held up one finger dramatically and walked into the den. After pacing in front of the bookshelves he came back with a photo album and set it on the kitchen table. He opened it to a photo of the old house in Brooklyn. Then he flipped backward a few pages until he stopped on a picture of Jenny and Phyllis and a young boy standing in front of an old truck.

"Who are those people?" Phillip asked.

"Well, that's your mother, and her sister—your Aunt Phyllis," Samuel said.

"Who's the boy?"

Samuel looked out into the other room to make sure no one else was stirring. "That's Noah," he said.

"Who's Noah?"

"He was . . . your mother's best friend," Samuel answered, remembering his son.

It was the photo that Phillip would not see again until fifty years later, while cleaning out his mother's house after she died, when Aunt Phyllis told him about his long-dead uncle Noah. It was the key to understanding Jenny; but in Florida Phillip had no idea that it was the key, or that there was even a door, or that the door would prove to be locked for decades.

"I don't want to live in Florida, Papa. I'm going to stay in our house forever," Phillip said. "I love our house."

"You can do that," Samuel said. "But you also have lots of time to change your mind if you want to. You don't have to decide right now." Then he pointed to the photo with one hand and put the other gently on the back of Phillip's head. "Try to remember that picture," his grandfather whispered, and then went looking in the kitchen cabinets for the box of Mallomars. Samuel had read all about Pavlov and the dogs.

Part Six

Patrick Elliot

CHAPTER TWENTY-THREE
James McKenna

PATRICK ELLIOT WAS THE last of the children born to James and Patricia Elliot of Rockville Centre, formerly of Dublin (and James formerly of Ballydraiocht), Ireland. As number six, behind Jack, he was coddled by his sisters and mostly ignored by his brothers, who wreaked havoc near and far, including ER visits for swallowing the tiny plastic sheep that went along with the Matchbox farm truck and letting the air out of the tires of the music teacher from the elementary school. Patrick grew up doing whatever he pleased whenever he thought of it—like an amiable ghost who happened to inhabit the house with the rest of them.

He never felt fully at home on Long Island, and didn't understand that he was homesick for someplace he'd never been. When his father told stories about Ireland Patrick always listened carefully, as if clues were being meted out. He imagined the rolling green land full of friendly eccentrics—farmers and fiddlers, storytellers and harmless, amusing drunks—and longed to live in such an agreeable place.

Friendliness, in fact, became Patrick's own defining characteristic. He loved people and found humor and warmth in them even when they behaved badly. His da liked to say that he was more optimistic than a deathbed priest.

By the time he reached high school Patrick's siblings had scattered to Manhattan and the outer edges of the outer boroughs. Only Jack was still puttering around the house—waiting to begin his military service—and the two grew close. Jack became Patrick's official coach in matters having to do with sports in particular and life in general.

But in the sport of golf, the student soon outshone his teacher. Patrick possessed a natural aptitude when he started playing as a lark at around age twelve, hitting balls in the field behind the high school when the soccer team wasn't playing there and learning to putt on a damp carpet in the Elliot backyard. When Jack began taking him to the driving range out on Rockaway Turnpike and the par-three course at Bay Park, Patrick's skills rose to the surface the way red color came into his cheeks when he was excited or embarrassed or when he exerted himself.

When Patrick was a high school junior and Jack had finished his final year as quarterback on the high school football team, Jack's coach called Patrick on the telephone one evening.

"I didn't do it, Mr. Steiner," Patrick said when he got on the line.

"What is it you didn't do?" the coach asked.

"Whatever it is you're calling about."

"You mean the golf tournament?"

"What golf tournament?"

"The one I was going to invite you to play in . . . ?"

"I'm sorry, sir, I haven't any idea what you're talking about."

"I can see that," Coach Steiner said. "So can I talk now before you continue playing defense?"

"Yes sir, of course."

"Your brother tells me that you're quite the golfer. I wouldn't accept that from most brothers but Jack's such a good athlete himself I trust his judgment. There's a charity tournament coming up at the Lawrence Golf Club this weekend. One of our group just dropped out and your brother says you're pretty handy with the wedge and putter."

"The driver, too!" Patrick said in an unusual moment of self-promotion. "But I've not played much competitively." Which was an exaggeration since he always played competitively against Jack; he had to give his brother three strokes per side to make their matches fair. They played for chores around the house. Patrick hadn't done his own laundry in months. Most of his underwear was pink.

The coach said, "There's a prime rib buffet after the golf, and the teams that do well take home some nice prizes."

While Patrick was happy to hear about Knicks tickets and original artwork and dinner for two at La Tavernetta, the words "prime rib buffet" won the day.

On the morning of the tournament Jack dropped Patrick off just beyond the parking lot of the Lawrence Club, where the other players were unloading their over-sized tour bags, which were whisked by assistant golf pros onto carts lined up in front of the clubhouse. The day was sunny and cool. Patrick could smell the salt air blowing in from the marshes and the yacht club adjacent to the golf course. He considered his skinny canvas carry bag with dismay.

Patrick found the scramble format of the tournament laughably easy—he'd never played a match where hitting an occasional duck hook or topping your tee shot didn't matter as long as one of your teammates kept his ball in play. The rules—and his teammates—encouraged Patrick to swing hard and take some chances, which he did to great success. His foursome chose eight of Patrick's drives to use, and he chipped in for birdie on a long, difficult par four and made several putts outside of ten feet. His team came in third and Patrick received enough credit in the pro shop to buy a new golf bag and a set of wedges. He also won a raffle prize—a love seat from the local La-Z Boy franchise, which his brother found hilarious. Patrick appeared genuinely surprised at every success in the tourney, which endeared him to his partners, who invited him to play in a small money game at the club the following Friday. Coach Steiner offered to cover anything Patrick lost during the first week as he figured out the various bets.

Jack encouraged him to accept the invitation. "There's a lot of rich and influential people at the club," he said. "You might meet someone who could be helpful to you."

"Helpful to me how?" Patrick asked.

"How would I know?" Jack said.

"What would I wear?" Patrick asked.

"Well, pants for starters. Probably a shirt, too, otherwise you're likely to be cold and you'll attract too much attention with those boobs of yours." Jack poked him in the chest.

"I don't have golf shoes. All the men in the tournament had golf shoes. I was the only player wearing PF Flyers."

"And you still played great. They don't care what you're wearing. They just want to win the big hitter's money."

"Which would be my other hesitation, since I don't have any," Patrick said. Which wasn't exactly true, as he'd been working in the hardware store in Rockville Centre a couple of afternoons a week, saving up for, well, he didn't know what for, except that it might give him some options at some point.

"Let the coach invest in you the first week. If you lose, don't go back. If you win, pay him back the entry he laid out for you and use the rest to fund the following week."

Patrick nodded. It seemed a solid financial plan. As long as their father didn't find out.

———

When he arrived at the Lawrence Club on Friday afternoon it was clear some of the other players had been drinking—which surprised him given that there'd be wagers riding on every hole. And that it was barely after twelve. How much money was riding he had no idea— Coach Steiner wouldn't tell him. There were so many different bets wagered simultaneously that one man joked that they only invited him to play because he was an accountant.

They proceeded in uneven groups of five or six, and when one group caught another on a green or tee box sometimes the players switched groups, so that Patrick could not track what was happening. He simply played his own game—consistently efficient, with occasional heroics, such as when he hit from a fairway bunker to three feet from the pin, to a smattering of applause. He nursed a single Miller High Life through the round because he didn't want to appear prudish about drinking even though he was not of legal drinking age. When somebody handed him a flask, he tilted his head back to appear like he was taking a hearty draught, but put his tongue over the opening.

On the back nine Patrick faded one of his tee shots toward the right rough, beyond a bunker and into a small grove of low trees. As he was walking in search of his errant Spalding Red Dot he saw one of the other players nudge his own ball out of the bunker with what Jack would have called a "foot wedge." Patrick looked away, but it got him to thinking. He hit his own shot onto the green and made the putt for birdie because it was the best chance of still beating the cheater on the hole so it wouldn't be an issue and he might be able to let go of it.

In the bar after the round, as the sun dropped toward Cedarhurst and Woodmere and Hewlett in a horizontal orange line, Mr. Steiner came up to him with a second Miller High Life.

"That first one must be pretty warm and flat by now," the coach said. Coach also handed him a wad of crumpled bills adding up to $220. It was the most money in cash that Patrick had ever seen.

"I can't take that, coach," Patrick said.

"You earned it, young man," the coach said, pressing it into his hand.

"There's something else, sir," Patrick said.

Coach signaled the barman, who brought him a tall glass of tonic and lime. "What is it, son?" he asked, looking over Patrick's shoulder.

"It's about Mr. Bauer," Patrick said. "I'm not accusing him or anything . . ."

"He cheats," the coach said. "We all know that. Every week someone is in charge of monitoring his real score. But I appreciate you mentioning it. That was the right thing to do. And he'll never know you said anything."

Still, the incident unnerved Patrick. He didn't return to Lawrence for the Friday game, although he worried that the other men might be angry that he'd taken their money and never come back. Like a hustler. He considered dropping by the coach's office and returning his winnings.

A few weeks later the coach called him at home.

"I don't think that game is for me," Patrick said.

"Yes, I gathered that when you stopped coming. But now can I tell you what I'm calling about?"

"I'm happy to return the money," Patrick said, although he wasn't exactly happy to. But he knew it would ease his conscience.

"Not possible," the coach said. "What I wanted to tell you is that some of the members were wondering if you're considering golf as a potential career?"

"You mean like being a golf pro?" Patrick asked. "Like, at a golf club? I never really thought about it."

"No, at the Royal Opera. Of course at a golf club," the coach said. "What plans *do* you have? In case you ever graduate from high school? Because there's an opening for an apprentice at Lawrence and I've been asked to find out if you'd like to apply."

"I don't have any plans," Patrick said, mulling.

"Which doesn't surprise me, son," the coach said. "Why don't you drop by the bag room Sunday afternoon and the attendant can explain a few things. And the members chipped in and bought you a pair of FootJoys."

Patrick started the job in the summer before his senior year. At first his responsibilities included hosing down the golf carts, pulling the flagsticks from the holes before dark, washing and setting out the range balls. Sometimes they'd send him to the hardware store for shower caulk, or out to fetch a few pizzas for a board meeting. He often got to hit balls at the practice range or play a few holes on the course if he came in early or stayed late and the tee sheet wasn't too full. Sometimes a member would invite him for a game.

One hot Saturday afternoon a well-dressed woman came into the shop asking about lessons for her son. Her jewelry looked like a burden, and Patrick figured she was from Hewlett Harbor, what they might have called a trophy wife. He thought the phrase referred to a woman that you would want to mount. Which in this case was also true.

The other pros were all busy—or too hot, or just too lazy—and one said that if her son was a beginner Patrick could offer a few basics and watch the boy swing.

Out on the range the boy held the club like a Louisville Slugger. Patrick showed him the interlocking grip, called the Vardon, after a famous nineteenth century British Open champ who favored it.

"It's so uncomfortable," the boy complained.

"It's not meant for comfort," Patrick said. "But you'll use it anyway. There aren't any great golfers who use the baseball grip. Then again there aren't any homerun hitters who use the Vardon Grip. But that's another matter."

He was a natural instructor—patient but persistent, funny in a dry way that kids liked. The mothers loved him, too. He was a hands-on teacher, holding the golf club over the grip of a student to demonstrate what the fingers should look like on the shaft, where the leather should cross the fatty part of the palm near the thumb. After a few months giving beginner's lessons he began working with the Lawrence High golf team on the weekends, running clinics and practice sessions.

Every now and then he'd see Coach Steiner at the club and greet him heartily.

"I'm grateful for your bringing me in, coach," he said one day, breathless with the emotion of it and the unfamiliarity of sharing his feelings.

"My pleasure. Coach," the coach replied.

When Patrick was in the final part of his apprenticeship to become a golf professional the members invited him to help out on a week-long golf trip they were planning to Ireland. They needed someone to drive the van while they drank in the back, and to sort their clubs and hotel arrangements. And maybe help out with a quick lesson if any of the players developed the shanks or the yips.

This was the same year his brother Jack stopped writing from Vietnam, and Patrick was hesitant—superstitious, almost—to join the trip and leave home at such a time. He felt he was somehow protecting his brother by keeping to his own normal routines. He wondered what Jack would have advised, and recognized his brother would have told him to go. In a recent letter from Vietnam Jack had mentioned how traveling, even in war, had revealed things to him. Wonderful things.

Patrick had grown tall and stocky and handsome, with a defined jawline and long, strong arms. He was polite and funny and people enjoyed being around him. He was the ideal golf valet for eight Lawrence members who planned to play at least eighteen holes per day—and he'd be welcome to play with them any time another player bowed out, or he could play by himself or with a local as long as he kept up with his required tasks. They'd pay all his expenses plus his normal club salary. He added three days onto the junket to visit his father's family in Ballydraiocht.

The trip was a revelation—not only because he'd barely been farther from home than the Jersey Shore, but because for the first time Patrick felt he'd found a place where he belonged. The singsong accents of the locals were musical and familiar to him. The soft green hills rising beyond fields dotted with sheep were like a painting he remembered from childhood and hadn't seen in a while, even though he'd never seen a painting like this. Patrons and workers alike at clubs and hotels and pubs often mistook him for a native. His travel companions joked that Patrick had enjoyed a secret life in Ireland before they'd all arrived.

Patrick drove them into Ballydraiocht as the last stop on their itinerary. His members played their final round on Ballydraiocht's Old Course, a short links venue with wide ocean views. One of the group had left earlier that morning so Patrick joined the others for the round.

On the sixth hole Patrick hit a tee shot high up into the marram grass left of the fairway and when he climbed to look for his ball and crested the hill, the view of the curving bay below, the round ruins of an ancient castle out on a rocky point, and the waves of the North Atlantic beyond clenched up his heart. He thought: this must be how ancient explorers—or Odysseus—felt returning home after a long voyage.

At The Whinging Lion following the round, the barkeep nodded to him with unspoken familiarity. While his American compatriots clinked glasses and boasted about their best shots, Patrick parked on a bar stool, taking it in: any of these local folk might be his cousin or uncle, he thought. Perhaps his grandparents had frequented this very bar—perhaps they were here even now.

Which they weren't, but he'd only missed them by about an hour.

Chapter Twenty-Four

Lager and Grapefruit

Patrick met his paternal grandparents for the first time at the same pub the next evening. Outside, two letters were burned out on the RESTAURANT sign so that it read: REST RANT. Patrick was unsure which directive to follow.

Rory and Margaret Elliot appeared older than Patrick had expected of folks barely into their sixties, but they were sturdily put together despite the lines on their ruddy faces etched from years of wind and sun and rain. His grandfather's grip was the kind you'd use trying to hit a one-iron out of long grass. His grandmother hugged him in the same careful, non-committal way that his own father always did.

Rory and Margaret wanted to hear everything about family back in the United States, about how their son—Patrick's father—had fared there, and what life was like for the American grandchildren, none of whom they had seen in many years, although photos of the entire U.S. Elliot clan hung in their cottage.

"We've always meant to come over to see you all," Margaret explained, looking down into her shandy.

"Life's proved full up for us right here," Rory added. "We've twelve grandchildren in the surrounding villages."

"And Rory's still sheeping and farming," Margaret added.

"And golfing, I hear," Patrick interjected. "My dad still tells stories about your heroic exploits on the links."

"So he still exaggerates then. But aye, I can still play a fair game," Rory said. "As I hear you can, as well. It must run in the family. Nothing passes by without the locals noticing around here. They probably know which jam you've been spreading on your scones in the mornings."

More drinks were ordered and toasts raised, and many folks came to their corner table to meet the young Patrick and offer a few words, most of which he understood despite their thick accents and indecipherable allusions. When the lights came up just before eleven Rory invited his grandson out for a round of golf with a couple of the other club members the next morning, to be followed by a dinner with, as Patrick gathered, about four thousand cousins.

The locals saw in short order that the young American could play. And not just in that high-lofted, soft-landing American way. He intuited the low running shot and his touch around the tricky greens was delicate as a surgeon's.

"We ought to offer him the assistant professional's job," one of the geezers joked to Patrick's grandfather while they were standing on a tee box looking out toward the grey-green ocean. The salt mist blew in their faces with the bracing effect of a cold towel.

"Aye, it would be an act of international friendship," Rory replied.

"I'll take it," Patrick said then, and they laughed until they realized that he meant it.

"I've some things to tie up back home," Patrick said. "And I'll have to break this to my parents. But I could start in, say, two weeks?"

Maybe if he'd been headed for Scotland or England Patrick's parents would have raised an uproar. But the idea of their charming, directionless boy closing the loop back to their homeland had a ring of joyful inevitability.

For Patrick, his most important connection to New York—his brother Jack—was so tenuous now that he thought a year overseas might provide the time for his brother to finish his military tour and return to them. And perhaps Patrick would return then, too, after a brief foreign adventure. Plus he'd be following his brother's admonition in a letter a few months back that he should live abroad.

But Patrick sensed with the same conviction that taking the job in Ireland was the right move, that his brother was dead. To wait for him at home any longer would be an unbearable cruelty, and so forward motion—toward something, anything—might provide a distraction from the pain he was preparing for.

Jack's wife, Jenny—the Jewess—shared Patrick's growing sense that Jack was lost to them. They invited her over to James Senior and Patricia's house for a farewell dinner for Patrick, when his sisters Katherine and Deirdre were back in town. Patricia cooked a lamb roast and oven potatoes and there was much toasting and joviality on Patrick's behalf, but any time the vaguest reference to Jack arose his family steered the conversation in another direction. Did they feel that talking about him might bring ill luck? Jenny figured it for some Irish superstition; Patrick knew that it was too painful a subject for the Elliot clan to take on.

The dinner occurred early in the spring, when the trees had leafed out and crickets were chirruping their anticipation of summer. After dessert and a few drams of whiskey Patrick walked Jenny to her car. They sat on the hood for a while listening to the clattering of dishes from inside the house and the distant hum of a gas-powered mower. The air was dusted with pollen.

Jenny shook her head and looked at the ground. "I know he's dead," she said.

Patrick mistook her certainty for evidenced fact. "Have you had a letter, then?"

"No, nothing like that. I don't know if they even know it over there in Vietnam or Cambodia or wherever he is. But I'm certain that he's not coming back. I've given up hoping. It's been months since he sent even a postcard and that's not like him. I don't care how secret his mission might be."

Jenny was expecting an argument, which she might have gotten from any of the other Elliots, which is why she didn't mention this at dinner.

"I've known it, too," Patrick said, and he put his hand on hers on the warm metal of the car hood. It was meant as a gesture of comfort, but when her fingers gripped his he also knew it was something more.

"Let's take a drive," Jenny said.

He directed her to the Lawrence Club, then onto a narrow lane adjacent to two distant holes built out on the bay, at the farthest point from the clubhouse. He'd been there before with a girl and a flask of Jameson, but nothing much had happened. He knew that on a blanket spread in a bunker behind the green they'd be protected from wind while they could smell the salt and rot of the inlet; that stars would be bright, shielded from the light pollution of town.

They didn't love each other, but they had in common the thing they both loved most in the world, and the only way to connect to Jack now was through the other person closest to him.

Jenny initiated it and took the lead. She looked into Patrick's face and saw Jack's, the man she would love forever. In her pain, she thought this the best way to keep her husband alive for her, in case he was already travelling through the afterlife.

"I'm going to Ireland," Patrick said. "To live." It sounded as if he meant: in contrast to dying, like his brother. He was carrying out his own family legacy, both forward *and* backward. He knew he should have mentioned it sooner. "I've taken a golf professional's job in my parents' hometown."

"I wish you well there," Jenny said.

It was one of the last things she'd ever say to the father of her first child.

Part Seven

Phillip and Spencer

CHAPTER TWENTY-FIVE
The Midget

PHILLIP COULD NOT LET go of the Uncle Jumpy letter—just as he had not been able to let go of any mystery that ever drifted across his path: why the man got off below his floor in the apartment building, except when it was raining; what happened on the grassy knoll; was the walrus really Paul? How many record albums did Phillip play backward as a kid just in case they communicated secret messages if you knew how to look for them?

He started at the Portland Historical Society, housed on the shady Southwest Park Blocks. The nice man there referred him to the nearby Central Library—a beautiful 1913 Georgian Revival designed by Albert E. Doyle. Phillip nearly lost himself in wandering the library when he came upon the etched black granite stairs and the Alice in Wonderland bas-relief and other beautiful features.

When he remembered his purpose and got back to it, a helpful bespectacled librarian informed him that for many years Portland published a city directory providing information about specific street addresses, including who lived there. Unfortunately, it started in 1930. Additional bad news was that the entire city of Portland renamed and renumbered its streets between 1931-1933—creating the current five quadrants of the city. Phillip loved the idea of five quadrants—it reminded him of how his mother used to talk about the third half of a football game. It was irreverent in a way that amused him to be living in Portland.

On their next Zoom call Spencer asked, "What's new with the Uncle Chimpy mystery?"

"Uncle Jumpy."

"Yeah, him. I get that you found the letter. And it's cool in the way of finding something awesome in an old house—although a signed copy of The Declaration of Independence hidden behind a painting of fruit would have been even cooler.

"And I get that you own the apartment where the letter was found and want to know more. It's like how you have to know who killed the friend in *The Third Man* or why there's a giant demonic rabbit in *Donnie Darko*, or how they even made a film as bad as *Clue*. You want to solve the mysteries. I get that. But how come you were never more curious about New York when you lived there—about the Five Towns, or Manhattan, or even Poughkeepsie, where the monster of you was first created at college?"

"All good questions," Phillip said. "I'll be sure to let you know when I figure any of it out."

———

As he delved deeper into the mystery, Phillip discovered that his thinking on it was skewed from the start. He couldn't reconcile that the letter was dated 1857, but that county records he uncovered showed the building they found it in wasn't even built until 1892.

Then further tenaciousness revealed that 1892 was the date when Portland started keeping track of property taxes, so all structures built before then were listed as having been built in 1892. So while the eight-plex could have been older, he learned that the oldest existing house in Portland was the 1855 Tigard/Rogers house in Bridlemile, which wasn't really even *in* Portland. The oldest residence he could find on the East Side, where the eight-plex resided, was the James B. Stephens House built in 1864. So even the oldest buildings weren't old enough. Which undermined not just Phillip's logic, but his mental image of someone pulling a covered wagon up in front of the eight-plex in 1857.

So either the date on the letter was incorrect—and why would someone intentionally misdate a letter, but then again why would someone stick an unsent letter into a doorframe in an old apartment to begin with?—or the letter had been brought along with someone or found by someone and placed in this particular building where it was not actually written because if the date was to be believed (and was it?) this building didn't exist yet. He suspected that the letter was somehow meant for him at the same time that he feared it might be leading him even farther from what he needed to discover.

So Phillip began following a second, tangential trail to learn more about the eight-plex itself. Which sent him back to the library and the kindly research librarian who pointed him toward the city directory, where Phillip found the names of owners of the building (including one named, amusingly, Jackoff) and six of the renters living there in 1930, as well as their professions, which included a teamster, a teacher, and a mason. Which didn't shed any further light but was still compelling.

Phillip was nearly inspired to shop for school supplies, as he had back in Larchmont after his mother passed and he began Sherlocking the father mystery with the help of colored pens and a map with pins and stacks of Post-it notes at her house. He considered hanging a timeline on the wall of his and Marty's rental house; this conundrum required a similar process to the one he'd undertaken to track his mother's movements over the decades of her life, ultimately leading him to discover that Patrick Elliot—not Patrick's brother, Jack—was his dad.

Phillip realized that what he *really* wanted to understand in this particular puzzle was the instinct that led someone to give up everything in the world that was familiar to them to climb into a rickety wooden vehicle and ride over mountain ranges and deserts and frigging prairies and God knew what other unknowns along the Oregon Trail, fighting Indians and calling food "vittles" and losing poor, sickly Albert in Nebraska?

Or what instinct led Phillip's own father, as another example, to leave his home on Long Island for another, greener island that he'd never seen, to eventually marry an Irish woman and live the rest of his life there? Or—as Spencer might suggest—how someone ended up suddenly living in Portland, Oregon, after half a century in New York, to cite another case. Just to start all over again.

Was it as simple as the idea of "wonderful things?" as his mother had promised? Sure, Portland was wonderful, but he was hoping for something more.

Could it have been that the searching itself was the point—that his mother knew that any search would teach him something about something, and the idea was to always be on a quest just to see where it might lead?

For fuck's sake, he hoped not.

Chapter Twenty-Six

Two Masters

On the other side of the planet (or at least 1/3 of the way around it), Spencer continued to chase castles in the sky despite suspecting this was a false quest. Literally, as many of the Irish castles he visited were built on high promontories. He wondered whether he was doing so as per the lyrics of Marty Robbins ("livin' in a castle in the sky"), or The Doobie Brothers ("surrounding castles in the sky") or Johnny Mathis ("building big castles in the sky") or High School Musical ("with wings to fly to his castle in the sky") or after the album by the French band The Airplane. Of course this wasn't to be confused with other bands named for aircraft, such as Jefferson Airplane or The B52s or the Fabulous Thunderbirds, or even The Foo Fighters, if you considered UFOs to be airplanes, or, possibly, Joan Jett. And that wasn't even taking into account bands that had recorded songs named for airplanes, such as Led Zeppelin's (and was a led zeppelin a kind of aircraft, he wondered?) "Sopwith Camel"; or with airplanes in the title, such as "Leavin' on a Jet Plane," written by John Denver but also performed by Peter, Paul, and Mary, or Suzy Bogguss's "Outbound Plane," or "Drunk on a Plane," by Dierks Bentley or for a real stretch, Kool and the Gang's "Higher Plane."

While Spencer was still pursuing his plan to visit an Irish castle each week—whether it was in the sky or not—in the hopes of somehow even accidentally fulfilling his mother's quest, the bulk of his attention turned to golf, which he believed also had secrets to reveal. He'd read *Golf in the Kingdom*, and while he didn't really understand it, the book's mysticizing of the game rang true in some way he hoped to eventually get. Golf was as old as many of the castles he visited. He also recognized that he wouldn't have found golf again as a serious subject of study if he hadn't travelled away from home.

"I'm taking lessons. From Patrick," he told his brother on Zoom.

"Patrick my father?" Phillip asked.

"No, Patrick the Prince of Darkness. Yes, your father. But also my wife's father, you might recall."

"I hope they're going better than that first lesson you took with him. You know—the one where you almost punched an eighty-year-old man who was trying to help you . . ."

"Oh, that's all behind us. Patrick loves me now. And not just because I married his daughter. I'm one of his best students. I started listening to his advice and he seemed to like that."

"And how's your game?"

"Vastly improved. I'm like a golf savant. I'm like Seve Ballesteros."

"You mean because you both share Spanish ancestry?"

"Yes, but also because we're handsome in that dark Mediterranean way."

"Are you keeping a handicap?"

"I am. It's twelve right now but Patrick thinks I can get into single digits. I've shot under 80 a couple of times. Did I mention I'm a golf savant? Like Miguel Angel Jimenez, and Rafa Cabrera Bello and Jose Maria Olazabal? I'm thinking I should have a third name like they do. Like Spencer Olazabal Elliot."

"You just like to say 'Olazabal' don't you?"

"Who doesn't? I'm playing several times a week. Trisha has won $43,000 Euros from me. I seem to have a gambling problem."

"Yeah—losing, apparently."

"I offered Patrick extra lesson fees if he would help me screw up Trisha's game, but he didn't accept."

"Perhaps because he's her father."

"I hate to admit it, but there's something to this whole golf thing," Spencer said. "I'd probably say it's transcendent if I knew what that meant. It's a kind of quest, if you think about it . . ."

––––––––––––––

The better Spencer got at golf, the more interested he became in it, until his interest became obsessive. At that level, the game became revelatory.

One day playing Ballydraiocht's new course with Patrick and a couple of other local codgers, Spencer was 240 yards from the green on a par five that rolled between steep hills and curved to the left just in front of the putting surface. He took out his one-iron—he only carried a one-iron because nobody on the planet has used one since the advent of modern technology. He took a mighty swipe at his ball and launched a low screamer that started on the right edge of the rough and flew like a Scud missile with a slight draw that brought it across the fairway just as the fairway turned, and it landed on the short grass and rolled another forty yards onto the green.

"Holy shit, I just fucking got it!" he shouted at Patrick, who watched the shot with amusement. "Did you see that? The elusive low running draw?"

"I did, yes," Patrick said. "I was standing right here."

"I finally figured out the secret: You have to swing outside to inside to hit that shot," Spencer said.

"Coincidentally, that's what I've been telling you for about seven weeks now. It's how you hit a low running draw."

"But now I figured it out myself," Spencer said.

The old man nodded. "You're half a genius, aren't you lad?" he said.

"I am at that. I'm finally solving a mystery. But what's the other half of me?"

"I'm a golf professional, not a zoologist," Patrick said, smiling into the wind.

Chapter Twenty-Seven
Or Barney Greengrass

PHILLIP AND MARTY WERE having dinner at Coquine up on the edge of Mount Tabor. They'd discovered the restaurant by accident on one of their long Southeast neighborhood walks. Coming down from the summit one evening they'd seen a line of people waiting to get in. As far as Phillip could tell, Portlanders didn't wait on line for restaurants, so he figured this one must be good.

Their meal there was so memorable that they also booked the next available evening, three nights later. They ordered the tasting menu with wine pairings. Half the dishes Phillip would never have chosen—halibut with licorice, seaweed, morels, and turnips; a pumpkin/faro concoction—but he loved every one. Coquine's offerings changed frequently, depending on what the chef found in the markets, or the forest, or what had recently been caught in the ocean, or maybe she employed tarot cards or rooster blood or tea leaves to identify what to cook on a given evening. Whatever her methods she was gifted, and dinner there became a weekly event, in much the same way that Phillip and Marty had gone to Sal's on the Upper West Side every week when they were first married the first time—where they'd peruse the entire menu but always order the chicken scarpariello.

Wine was a particular revelation at Coquine, and Phillip was trying to educate himself about an entire viticulture region he'd never given much thought to while living on the east coast: the Willamette Valley. The restaurant's sommelier was able to make every tasting note sound like a mini telenovela filled with intrigue and romance, despite that almost all of the characters were grapes.

They sipped an ice-cold mineral-forward auxerrois from Bjornson Vineyards and watched birds settle in the old-growth firs above them. They'd just learned to identify old-growth firs. Every day there was something.

Phillip was wearing a blue and white lumberjack shirt untucked over Prana jeans—a loose new look for him. Marty was in tight black toreador pants and a rosewater silk shirt, still a New York look, but one that Phillip felt suited her sophisticated beauty even in the Pacific Northwest. Her only nod to their new surroundings was a wildness to her curly hair.

"I'm thinking about going fishing with the boys next weekend," Phillip said after the waiter slid an elf-sized portion of Gragnano bucatini in brown butter in front of them.

"I didn't realize they had a Zabar's here," Marty said. "Are you going for lox or sable?"

"That's funny," Phillip said, tilting his wine glass at her. They watched the legs of the wine sliding down the inside of his glass.

Marty smiled, enjoying that her husband was enjoying her. This second marriage to Phillip was much improved. Was this to do with where they found themselves now, in Portland, or to Phillip having matured, or that his mother was dead, or to other factors? She didn't know. But what mattered was that they were in love again.

"The boys invited me to stay at their cabin at Black Bart's Ranch." "The boys" is how Phillip had begun referring to his three partners in the eight-plex.

"I think it's Black *Butte* Ranch, sweetheart," Marty said.

"Yeah. Black Butte." He knew it was Black Butte but it was fun to say "Black Bart's." It sounded like the hideout of the bad guys in the western Phillip sometimes fancied he was living in. "They go fishing there. It can't possibly be interesting—the fishing—but it seems like a good way for me to get to know them a little better."

"Maybe you'll like the fishing. You liked the rafting trip in Idaho. You're becoming a regular Arnie Bauer."

"Eddie Bauer," Phillip laughed.

Marty nodded. She knew it was Eddie Bauer.

The following Friday Phillip drove to Black Butte with Trevor Buxton, the senior-most of his new partners. Meaning he was thirty-one. Trevor was tall and athletic with a beard curated to always look three-days old. They listened to country music—Phillip was struck by a song about a man marrying his pickup—in Trevor's black BMW

SUV and talked about cap rates and cost segregation analysis and also the love they had for Craftsman details in old buildings. Phillip couldn't believe the ride went by so fast. He hadn't even noticed the firs giving way to stately ponderosa pines. The dark, rocky dirt higher up the mountain had turned red as they descended. Phillip hadn't yet learned to identify ponderosa pines—which he'd later recognize smell like butterscotch.

Trevor's "cabin" was actually a five-bedroom, seven-bath log-frame home with a great room built out of man-sized river rock and a professional kitchen off a redwood "smoking" deck sporting a built-in brick Forno Bravo pizza oven. Overlooking the golf course.

When Phillip had asked earlier in the week what kind of food he could bring, Trevor said the chef would take care of everything, Picturing a tiny wood-frame cabin crowded with bunk beds and covered in tar paper, Phillip imagined that Trevor was referring irreverently to himself as "the Chef." But when they arrived, Mikey—an actual chef—was buzzing around the giant kitchen doing prep work for what looked like a holiday dinner. A three-bone rib roast was waiting to go into the Wolf oven. Romaine and eggs and anchovies and fresh garlic were ready to be combined into a Caesar salad. A charcuterie board the size of a manhole cover was assembled on a sanded and stained stave from a wine barrel on the granite countertop next to a small army of local pinot noirs.

After dinner the boys went off to fetch their fishing gear and then reconvened on the deck. It was still light at eight, a syrupy gold moving slowly through the trees and across the green grass of the fairway just beyond the property line. They took Phillip out on the fairway and gave him his first casting lesson, using a hula-hoop as his target.

They competed with each other to offer what each thought was the most crucial information about fishing, almost all of which was lost on the New Yorker. It was hard to say which party took greater amusement from the session—except when Phillip hooked Trevor's hat and zipped it through the evening air.

―――――――――

Despite drinking bourbon and smoking thick Romeo Y Julieta 1875 Reserve Maduros to welcome the perfumed darkness that night, the boys were all up before six the next morning, sipping strong French roast and eating breakfast sandwiches on the back deck. They were wearing waders and considering boxes of trout flies laid out on the table before them.

"Just to be clear," Phillip said, "I have no idea what any of this stuff is, or how it works, or where I'm supposed to throw it in a river, as opposed to throwing it at a hula hoop on a golf course. Where I noticed there weren't very many fish at all. Or what to do if by some miracle I catch one."

"Oh, you won't catch a fish," Mitchell—the most taciturn of the young partners—said. "We almost never do."

"He's only partly joking," Trevor said. "The Metolius is one of the toughest trout streams in the country."

"Is that what we're fishing for?" Phillip asked.

"You'll have to go to the Deschutes River if you want to catch a steelhead," Darren said.

"Okay," Phillip said. "Good to know. Not that I have any idea what a steelhead is."

"They're trout who think they're salmon," Trevor said. "They're born in freshwater streams then journey out to the ocean for a few years of foreign travel before returning home to spawn."

"And either you'll *get* fishing or you won't," Mitchell said. "And if you do . . ."

"It's game over," Trevor said.

They drove the eight miles to Camp Sherman with the kind of boyish anticipation Phillip remembered from trips into Manhattan when he was nineteen, or how it felt when the team bus was pulling into the opposing team's campus for a college soccer match, or when he was picking up a date that he hoped might give him a hand job.

Mitchell and Darren jumped out of the vehicle before Trevor shut off the engine and disappeared upstream with their gear. Trevor spent the next few minutes tying tiny brownish-green flies onto his own and Phillip's lines. He handed Phillip a pair of patched waders and showed him what was in each of the pockets of the vest he'd loaned him: 5x and 6x fishing line; a tiny bottle of floatant; drop shot weights; thingamabobbers; and a small waterproof box of weed.

"This is right out of the Norman Maclean novel," Phillip said. "Except for the weed."

"Just don't be the idiot with the hooker who sunburns his privates," Trevor said.

Phillip was gladdened that his partner/fishing coach knew the reference.

Trevor spent another twenty minutes explaining the logistics of the river and where the elusive trout might be hiding. He pointed to "bomb shelters" where the fish hid in deep pools, and how these were often behind big boulders, as well as "feeding lanes" where the fish might pop out to grab a quick snack.

"It's like they've got their own underwater domiciles, with all the comforts of home for eating and sleeping and whatever else they do down there," Trevor said. "I'll be within a hundred yards if you need anything. My advice is to find a place where there's a lot of room behind you, where you won't lose your fly in a tree on the first back cast. And try not to fall down and drown."

Phillip lost his fly in a tree on his first back cast, after which he spent ten minutes following the line back and climbing up into the low branches and surgically removing the hook from the bark. And then unbefuckering the line. And falling down. But not the drowning part.

He waded back into a shallow part of the river, trying not to step in over his head. He'd been told to avoid surprising the fish, but he couldn't tell if they were joking about that part. The clarity of the water mesmerized him. He watched the rounded stones below, in every color and shade from white to brown to purple, trailing green scarves of algae. The trees around him soughed and swayed in an upriver breeze.

After a short while the motion of casting became more natural as he stopped thinking consciously about his hands moving in an arc from ten o'clock to two o'clock; as he felt the line loading behind him, and then snapped it forward, and heard the zinging of the filament with its hook on the end, until the fly drifted back into sight and settled on the surface. The motion was hypnotic, and the sound of flowing water tranquilized him.

Trevor had given Phillip a size-sixteen spotted sedge so he could see where his casts landed. Once or twice the fly dipped below view and he thought possibly a fish was nibbling at it in some nether world, but when it happened in the same spot several times he realized the current was dragging the fly down. He figured out how in the eddies on the edge of the current the river flowed back upstream. He was like a kindergartner confronted with his first opportunity to learn, say, that coffee was hot, or that adults didn't like to talk about their feelings, and the compounding revelations threatened to overwhelm him. He was relaxed but hyper aware in a way he'd not experienced as an adult without the help of drugs.

Some time later Phillip eyed the other three men walking back downstream toward the car along the path beside the river. Trevor waved him over.

"Are you guys done already?" Phillip asked. He was just starting to get the hang of this thing.

"Lunch time," Trevor said. "And you don't want to miss Chef Mikey's calzones."

"Lunch? We just ate breakfast," Phillip said.

The others looked at each other, laughing and nodding their heads. "That was four hours ago," Trevor said.

Chapter Twenty-Eight

Gravity?

Spencer and Trisha were having a drink in the Ballydraiocht club-house bar after golf. It had been a half sunny, windy, warm day on the links and they were both tired and invigorated by the round. Trisha wore her red hair in a ponytail tucked through the back of her green golf hat with the Rovers logo on it.

"Has my da mentioned The Tournament of Relativity to you yet?" she asked as they clinked glasses and looked each other in the eye—an officially proper toast.

"I don't think so. I'd probably remember that," Spencer said. He pushed his modified Hogan style ivy cap to the edge of the table so there was nothing but frothy Guinness between him and his wife.

"It's an annual club event where you put together a foursome of a women's club golfer, a senior, a men's club member, and a guest. But each one of them has to be related to at least one of the others. It's the social event of the summer here."

"Well that must really be saying something," Spencer said. "So two foursomes participate?"

She swiped at him with her golf glove. "Da was going to ask you to play with us this year."

"But then he saw how my lessons are progressing?" Spencer took her hand across the table. He rubbed her gold wedding band with one finger, maybe reveling in it a little.

"Nah. The opposite. He said you're one of the best twelve handicaps in the county, currently. But that when your handicap drops you'll never be able to sustain it. So the time for you is now."

"Ah," Spencer said. "So you're all just riding me. Like a pony."

"It's been our nefarious plan all along," Trisha said.

"Hey, *I* say 'nefarious plan.' You can't just use that phrase whenever you feel like it."

"It wasn't in the prenup," Trisha said. "You'll have to talk to my solicitor."

The Relativity Tournament took place two weeks later. The wind blew a force three gale (not really, but Spencer liked to use the phrase "force three gale") and anyone wearing a golf cap had to switch to a watch cap so their headgear didn't end up in Portugal. Old Patrick was thrilled by the conditions.

"This is what we've been training for," he said to Spencer in the locker room as they were pulling on wind shirts over their golf shirts, despite it being summer. Padraig and Trisha were already out on the practice range hitting perfect low runners into the blue Irish sky.

"I thought we were required to have a senior golfer on our team," Spencer said, and the old man smiled.

"You probably didn't know that we get extra strokes for every year the senior member is above seventy-five," Patrick said.

"That's nearly a stroke a hole for you," Spencer joked.

Patrick took hold of the wooden door of his locker, steadying himself. "Just make sure you point me in the proper direction on each of the tee boxes."

"That reminds me," Spencer said. "I have a very old friend who likes to play golf . . . but he's got Alzheimer's now."

"Is that right? Which friend would that be?"

"Why do people always ask 'which friend?' My friend Jimmy, okay? He still plays every week, with his pal Johnny, who's blind."

Patrick nodded. "And how does that work out for them, then?"

"Well," Spencer said, making the motion of shooting his cuffs even though he was wearing a shirt without any cuffs, "When they step up on the tee, Jimmy—he's the one with dementia—points Johnny, the blind guy, down the middle of the fairway . . . like you just asked me to do for you today. Then Johnny hits his drive and says, 'Did you see it, Jimmy?'

"And Jimmy usually says, 'Yeah, I saw it.'

"'Well, where did it go?' Johnny asks.

"'Where did what go?' Jimmy says."

Patrick snorted a laugh. "I'll be using that one with the boys," he said. "If I can remember it. I might have to explain it to the denser ones."

And off they went, an odd foursome of golfers who were even odder as family, playing as a team—celebrating each other's good shots, turning away as if they hadn't just seen the bad ones.

Padraig's game took a slight detour on the fifth hole when he hit two drives into a ravine that was marked as out of bounds. He'd engineered sidespin on the balls for a draw but when the wind caught them they took a ninety-degree turn instead of a soft curve.

"You can't win every hole, son," Patrick said to him as they watched the second one disappear. "It wouldn't be fair to the others."

Padraig was hard on himself. Spencer had seen this in golfers his whole life—guys who once they went south couldn't find their way north again. Spencer had observed that these players were usually so concerned that their playing partners would judge them as people based on the way they performed at golf that they failed to realize that they were actually being judged as people on how they *reacted* to the way they performed at golf. So a guy who could play badly but still manage to have fun was far more valuable a compatriot than a guy who played well most of the time but melted down emotionally on the rare occasions he didn't. Spencer was glad to see that Padraig was not one of those people.

But still: being hard on yourself was also a part of the game.

"You all carry on," Padraig said after the second tee shot went awry. "I've had enough on this hole. Perhaps I'll just go drown myself in the ocean." He swung his club back and forth in front of him.

"Do you think you can keep your head down that long?" Spencer said.

On the next hole it was Spencer's turn to bungle his drive on a short par four, topping it so that it bounced and dribbled out about 150 yards. He was committed to taking this in stride, and merely shrugged off the duffed shot. Padraig walked out to his ball with him—not a very far walk.

Spencer calculated he had about 190 yards to the green with a wind blowing hard from behind him and slightly from the left. He was also committed to playing fast, so he pulled a club out of his bag, then looked at Padraig.

"Think I can get there with a five-iron?" Spencer asked as he started to set up the shot.

"Eventually," Padraig said with that smile that looked like Phillip's.

Otherwise, Spencer performed well, hitting crisp shots that used the terrain to move his ball closer to the holes. There was a satisfaction in it that he couldn't explain—something deeper than sport was at work. After lofting a wedge shot over the edge of a burn and watching it check up on the green and nuzzle close to the pin he wondered for just a moment: is *this* my quest? Am I to learn something from *golf*, for fuck's sake? Is it meant to bring me closer to family? To enlightenment? Could this have been the sort of thing his mother was getting at? To his displeasure Spencer couldn't discount the possibilities.

Patrick and Trisha also played consistently all day, hitting greens in regulation and making par putts to keep their team on the leaderboard. But the old man was limping slightly down the fairways, leaning on his trolley; he paused to catch his breath after climbing up to some of the raised greens.

"You all right, Da?" Trisha asked him. She offered to push his trolley for him. Padraig was also solicitous toward his father, pulling clubs for him and, toward the end of the round, teeing up his ball when the old man had difficulty bending down.

"Might be a touch of the ague," Patrick said. "Not quite myself today."

"We're sorry to hear it," Spencer said. "Although I don't recall ever hearing anyone say the word 'ague' out loud before. It's particularly referred to as a symptom of malaria," he added, for no particular reason other than he knew that.

"I'm sorry to let you all down," Patrick said.

"Not a'tall, Da, not a'tall," Trisha said. "You're playing just fine, even if it doesn't feel like it." Which he was—on his way to shooting 74 on the day.

"We're just happy to be out here with you, Da," Padraig added. He put a hand on the old man's shoulder.

"And I'm lucky to be out here with all of you. Thank you for the invite," Spencer said, catching them off guard with a heartfelt comment.

Their team placed third in the competition and nobody seemed disappointed, although there was some concern for Patrick, who was less jovial than normal despite volleying back all attempts to send him home.

"You know I won't miss a banquet—especially one I've already paid for," he said.

In the bar afterward Spencer inquired as to whether any of them ever took caddies in competition—to let someone else worry about the bag and reading the yardages and the like. When he looked up from the table, he saw the champions board and the club presidents board hanging on the wall with the names of Elliots repeated many times: legacy in action, he acknowledged.

"In this family, we know the golf course better than the caddies do," Patrick said.

"And we know the caddies, as well," Trisha added, and they all nodded and smiled.

"They're a rough lot, here," Padraig explained. "It's the preferred career choice of professional tipplers."

"And they're a dentist's dream," Trisha added.

"Sometimes five or six of them share a set of uppers," Padraig said.

"That reminds me of a friend of mine who hired his first caddie ever on a trip to Ireland," Spencer said. "He'd just gotten off an overnight flight from New York and instead of heading for his hotel to sleep he figured he'd get on local time by playing eighteen holes first . . ."

"Let me guess—your friend Jimmy," Patrick said. He raised his Guinness to his mouth with a shaky hand.

"Exactly right!" Spencer said. "Well, as you could imagine, Jimmy was pretty knackered after the red-eye from New York.

"So he picked up a caddie who was hanging out in the parking lot of the club he was playing at, even though he'd never had a caddie before. After a while he wondered if the guy was even a real caddie. He ended up playing one of the worst rounds of his life—and he was a pretty good golfer, too. He told us that the bad golfing was mostly the caddie's fault—the old fellow misread all the greens, clubbed him badly, and failed to ever take wind into account when figuring how far to try to hit the ball. The more frustrated he became at the caddie the worse Jimmy hit even the easy shots, spraying and shanking them all over the course, and even whiffing at one on the tee box. He was beside himself.

"Finally on the back nine Jimmy hit a putt exactly as his caddie advised him and it rolled off the green into a pot bunker.

"'You've got to be the worst caddie in the world,' Jimmy screamed at the codger.

"And the caddie paused a long moment while he was cleaning

Jimmy's golf ball with a ratty towel, and said, 'Oh, I don't think so, sir . . . That would be far too great of a coincidence.'"

CHAPTER TWENTY-NINE
Beyond The Fairway

"I WENT FISHING," PHILLIP told his brother to open their next Zoom conversation.

"You so did *not* go fishing," Spencer said. "What's *wrong* with you? Now you're going to tell me you liked it. And that you bought a fishing pole—which you'll insist I refer to as a 'rod'—made from moonstone and spider legs, and that it gives you extra torque for the triple salchow or some such falderal. And that you bought rubber clothing and you're walking around with a fishhook wrapped in feathers in your hat."

"Falderal? Really?" Phillip said. "And the rod is graphite."

"Oh, how I would love to see this," Spencer said. "Don't take this personally, but could there be a stupider sport than this? I mean really. Standing in a freezing stream all day with a silly hat on . . . and a net, trying to trick a poor fish into eating fake food. It's like if you had a dog and you tapped on his bowl in the morning and he came running over but the bowl was full of feathers. With a fucking hook in the bottom."

"Who's Annette?" Phillip said.

"Annette?"

"You said standing in a stream with a silly hat and Annette. You know what fishing taught me?"

"That you need a different hobby?"

"That we're a lot like lox," Phillip said. He knew that would stop Spencer in his tracks for at least a moment.

"I'm listening."

"Well, at least we're like salmon, before they're smoked, and steelhead—and please don't tell me that I shouldn't be smoking."

"Ohhh . . . kayyy . . ."

"You probably know this already, being such a stable genius, but salmon are born in rivers and then swim out to the ocean and wander around for most of their lives, traveling the world. But they always return home eventually. Steelhead too. They're trout that do the same thing. And even more interesting is that the trout that travel are no longer even the same fish when they come back: they're changed! Their travels have changed them!"

"I see where you're going and I'd like to put a stop to this discussion before you compare us to cream cheese," Spencer said. "I don't get why you don't spend your valuable but apparently unlimited leisure time doing something more sensible than fishing—like golfing!"

"Ah, golfing. A sport that truly tests your physical abilities. A sport that includes a drink cart. Full of booze. And candy bars."

"They say 'drinks' cart over here. Which makes sense since the carts almost always have more than one drink. It wouldn't be very efficient otherwise."

"And how is the sport of fat, rich, white guys?"

"It's fine. But I have some not great news."

"You missed a three-foot putt?"

"You know as well as anyone that I hate to be serious. But Patrick's not doing so well. There's been some debate about whether to tell you or not, since you've only recently started your own new life as a frontiersman. I wanted to give you a heads up. But this is completely unofficial. You didn't hear it from me."

"How much not doing so well?"

"It's hard to say. He's ailing. He looks like he's 200 years old. It might be nothing."

"If it wasn't nothing, what might it be?"

"It might be cancer of some sort? There seems to be a wide variety but apparently none are 'the good cancer,' like with cholesterol. The family's not forthcoming with a lot of intimate details. Just like the way we were raised, coincidentally. I think there may be an oncologist involved, though, which is never what you want to hear."

"How are his spirits?"

"Well, his short game is pretty tight right now so he seems happy enough. But he's very tired."

"Is this your secret way of telling me I should come out there?"

"That part isn't meant to be secret. And just so long as you understand that it's not because I'm desperate to see you. Even though I might be . . ."

"That's a separate issue," Phillip said. "But back to the fishing. And the golfing. What *is* wrong with us?"

"I know. It's like if they made a movie combining *A River Runs Through It* with *The Legend of Bagger Vance* where Will Smith beats Brad Pitt senseless with a canoe paddle while Robert Redford voices over the whole thing and tells us it's religion."

Phillip paused. "Or maybe its like *Caddyshack* meets *The Old Man and The Sea*," he countered. "Where Spencer Tracy is dying of dehydration and then hooks Bill Murray and drags him back to Cuba while the cast of *Saturday Night Live* swims around the boat and Ted Knight yells, 'You'll get nothing and you'll like it!'"

"Hey, that's not bad," Spencer said

"They're such cliché sports, is what bothers me," Phillip said. "Like we're supposed to receive some kind of Zen revelation by catching a trout or sinking a stupid putt."

"Well, yes, at least the fishing is dumb, I agree . . . But I'm tired of the entire quest thing. If I was Odysseus I'd just make peace with the Amazons and stay on their island. I could help them sell the books."

"I don't think Odysseus ever met the Amazons. That's a different myth—maybe that was Hercules. But we seem to be following the themes of *The Odyssey* saga nonetheless. Even if our efforts are a little less heroic."

"What are the themes?

"From what I can remember: wandering, testing, omens, and return."

"So golf has all of that? I must be missing something."

"That's the thing: what are we missing? In this whole stupid search inspired by a known liar with dementia?"

"If we knew that, it wouldn't be missing," Spencer said. "But I like the idea of return."

CHAPTER THIRTY

Clarence

THE DEMOLITION OF THE Portland eight-plex continued without revealing any additional surprises other than some newspapers from the 1920s, most likely left during repair work, and a woman's shoe that looked to be from the Victorian era. Once everything had been removed from the building and loaded in the construction dumpster, Phillip's own workload increased. His vision and experience drove the project even though his partners had found the building. He imagined its renaissance in a sort of Victorian steam punk industrial aesthetic, with Edison-bulb lighting and exposed black metal ductwork and dark cabinets with metal mesh doors.

Which also meant that Phillip was responsible for showroom visits to pick out all the surface materials and paint colors. He and Marty spent their days carrying floorboards, and tile and marmoleum samples, and paint swatches all over town as they melded their choices together into an overall look. It was a good way to familiarize themselves with Portland's five quadrants.

Phillip worried about his new old father, and whether a moment was approaching when he'd need to make the trip back to Ireland. Which also meant that Uncle Jumpy was largely forgotten. Which answered the question of whether there were some mysteries Phillip could just let go of. He *liked* the idea of an unsolved puzzle that was not his responsibility to discover an answer to.

"Let's go back to Ireland while there's some time to be with Patrick," Marty mentioned one evening over pizza at Hot Lips, on Hawthorne. Phillip was surprised by how delicious the Sicilian slices were—though they called it "pan pizza"—with light, fluffy dough beneath layers of cheese and homemade pepperoni. Maybe as good as New York, though he would never admit that.

"It's so unexpected, even though it shouldn't be," Phillip said. "My father, that is, not the pizza. I just got him. I haven't even had time to get to know him. And now I may lose him."

Marty sipped at her grapefruity IPA from Barley Brown's, in far-off Baker City. The beer had travelled hundreds of miles to delight Portlanders.

"It makes me sad," Phillip said.

"It is sad," Marty agreed. "But also lucky. It's an opportunity you never saw coming. You have a whole new family you could still get to know. Ireland's beautiful, and we haven't seen much of it."

"But what about our new life here? What about being western pioneers and growing up with the country?"

"We can come back here and grow up any way we choose to," Marty said.

"I know." Phillip nodded grudgingly.

"What is it then?"

"We don't really have that much time ourselves," he said. "To keep starting the starting over. To keep looking for home. To go on quests even of our own choosing. To swim out to the ocean and then back again."

"There's no predetermined plot," Marty said then. "We can make it up as we go. We never anticipated the part where we're back to-gether. You never planned on having a father at this point in your life, or ending up in Oregon. We have a chance to revise the story line every day and do what we please, and if that doesn't please us, to do something else."

"I've decided to abandon Uncle Jumpy and family," Phillip said then. "It was a false trail. There's enough mystery in my own family for a lifetime. I'm just going to frame the letter and hang it in the lobby of the finished building. Like my brother suggested. Let it imply a story that people can make up their own conclusions about. Like I'm trying to do with my own life. If there's something to that letter, or to letters in general, it will reveal itself eventually."

They continued exploring the Oregon territory. They stayed at a famous river lodge so that Phillip could extend his streak of not catch-ing any fish. They climbed minor peaks and fell off mountain bikes in the high desert and drank pinot noirs wherever they were made.

They planned only as far ahead as a dinner reservation or a day hike in the Columbia River Gorge, where Phillip made up the names of wildflowers.

"That's a lemon doozy," he said, pointing at a Dalles mountain buttercup. "It gets the bloodstains of murder victims out of your clothes.

"And that's a purple fuck-all. It's poisonous," he said, indicating a broad-leaf lupine. "The only known antidote is to eat an entire apple pie without worrying about the calories, which no one can do.

"And that one . . ." he said, stopping to touch the delicate petals of the poet's shooting star, "That one is a crazy windmill flower. It actually creates energy that can be harnessed by woodchucks."

On the way home they stopped in Hood River for dinner. Walking along the downtown streets Phillip looked up at the vacant old red brick Waucoma Hotel, which had been closed since 1973.

"Don't even think about it," Marty said.

"It would make a great condo project . . ."

"Zip it," she said.

Phillip encountered people he liked while renovating the eight-plex—an architect he started to meet at a brewpub occasionally; his partners; a fellow former New Yorker he was paired up with on a rare golf round at Pumpkin Ridge Golf Club. Marty met women at her yoga studio up on SE 50th and had coffee with them, and was invited to join a book group where she met a few others. But the newlyweds also realized they were self-contained, unlike during their first marriage. They didn't need other people. They curled into each other and discovered a depth and complexity not unlike that of the new wines they were getting to know.

Some days Marty disappeared into the light-filled painting studio at the back of the house in the way that Phillip had fallen into fly fishing that first time; she'd discover that the sun had swung overhead and down the other side of the pitched roof without her noticing the passage of time. Other days, when Phillip visited the job site or met with his partners or bankers or architects, Marty would take a canvas and portable easel and head for Lone Fir Cemetery or venture across the river to the Lewis and Clark College campus or Tryon Creek Park, where she realized for the first time that fir trees smelled like fruit.

She was also discovering her own private depths without work to buffer her from her own personality and desires, although she wasn't certain yet whether this was due to their new locale, as Phillip posited, or the freedom from the old routine that her entire life had wrapped itself around like a soft, tight scarf for the past three decades. She was expanding at a rate she could barely track. She was a supernova. Days were exhilarating and sometimes scary for the open territory they encompassed; what would she do with all that empty space? Could she fill it without a job? Did she want to?

Marty was often brought back to her earlier years in Iowa—both when she lived out on the farm twenty-five miles from town and also the years when the family moved closer to Devine so she could play in the high school band and spend time with her friends instead of getting on the bus and driving through cornfields and soybean fields to be stuck out in the boonies afternoons and evenings. Her life grew full for the first time in those days when she was free of chores and could follow whatever interested her: boys, books, sports, the building of relationships and the training of her vision on things far beyond the horizon of church steeples and trees planted as wind breaks for a homestead on an otherwise empty stretch of prairie.

Spencer experienced his own move away from New York differently because he had the anchor of Trisha—although she didn't much care for that analogy. This was the best and also the most challenging part of his own adaptation: her roots in Ballydraiocht penetrated through the fescue and sand probably all the way down to the water table, and maybe lower. Maybe to the molten core of the planet. While the people he met were new to him, he was already connected to them through his wife. When he found what he thought of as a special place—a hidden cove with a narrow slice of beach, a bookstore in a town an hour away—it was only a revelation to him: Trisha already knew these places, so the sense of discovery was different. Except, of course, for the ones inside himself.

Those were subtle, and acknowledged only grudgingly: as one example, that he had not only a responsibility to think about someone else now—not just wandering off in some direction and forgetting to go home for dinner—but to consider her interests at all times. It clarified for him just how lousy a boyfriend he'd made over a very long period. But he also began to depend on Trisha in a way he hadn't ever let himself rely on anyone. He shared his fears of being away from New York and thus losing who he was.

"I'm struggling to create a new identity," he told her in the pub one night. "I'm like a crime boss who's been inaugurated into witness protection and has to get along in an alien environment without ever referencing the murderous shitheel he was before."

It was hard work and sometimes exhausting. Even the gregarious Spencer occasionally chose staying home over attending some pub event like trivia night (which he would have excelled at) or a darts competition, or even a jam session at some musician's spread outside of town.

And then, as suddenly as the funk of change had come down on him like a heavy stage curtain, he was free of it. Reenergized. Humorously annoying, which was his peculiar charm. He was done with running crazily down false trails with his hair on fire. He and Trisha went everywhere together. His new philosophy was: stop thinking and just say yes to every invitation. And so he sheared his first sheep, and the looks of fear and astonishment entertained half the village. He clogged at a talent night—but dressed as an Amish farmer in overalls and a fake beard, straw hat, a long blade of fescue in his teeth.

Even the band warmed to him and while they continued to resist his efforts to get them more gigs, he became de facto manager. He negotiated a higher pay scale—anything was higher than a few quid and free drinks—and got the pub to pay for production of a logoed sign that he designed. He undertook a major personal literacy campaign, including slogging through what had to be one of the longest—and heaviest—books ever written, about the history of Rome. He watched a thousand British police procedurals: each time a new character appeared he pointed and yelled "The dog's bollox: *That's* the murderer!"

The key to everything was that he was not waiting for anything. Maybe his mother was wrong about this one; maybe *that* was the revelation that freed him. He didn't expect or covet or encourage change, or intentionally set out to fit himself into the puzzle of Ballydraiocht. He did what he wanted, but only after quick calculations of how it might affect Trisha, or other people he was becoming close to in the small town. And this was the biggest change of all: with his shift in locale he became considerate. Released from a New Yorker's cynicism he discovered his own kindness.

And yet . . . and yet . . . The brothers were both New Yorkers down to their orthopedic structures. There were things they never stopped thinking about: steam rising from subway grates on a winter day, obscuring the pretzel vendor; aging, limping softball players in Central Park; the hushed formality of expensive restaurants; the freedom to have General Tso's chicken delivered to your door almost before you hung up the phone with the Chinese restaurant on the corner. Small stuff, but the stuff that lives were built around.

And the hardest part of each of them getting to know themselves in new ways in new places was that they didn't know what that meant to them as brothers who'd forged their relationship over board games and summer camp and memories of their mother, together in most things, knitted tightly by the absence of a father, each the other's protector, advocate, and critic.

One evening when Spencer and Trisha returned from dinner at Patrick and Lorna's he said, "I've got to show you something." They were having a wee dram on the porch. The night was dark and the lights from scattered cottages twinkled like the sparks from a lighter low on butane.

Trisha had learned to be wary of Spencer's reveals. "Will I be needing third-party verification for whatever you're going to show me?"

Spencer got up and went inside the cottage then came back with his phone and a deck of playing cards.

He pulled out the cards and shuffled them with a degree of mastery that didn't surprise her.

"Pick one," he said. He was nervous, as always.

She picked a card and showed it to him and Spencer punched a number into his phone.

In Southeast Portland Phillip fumbled for his own phone, woken from a nap, heart drumming wildly. He wondered who'd died.

"This is Phillip," he said, not having looked at the number of the incoming call.

"May I speak to Mr. Wizard?" Spencer said.

Phillip hesitated, remembering how this went.

"Clubs. Hearts. Spades . . ." he said deliberately.

"Yes, I can hold," Spencer interrupted—though Trisha didn't know

159

he was interrupting, had no idea what was happening on the other end of the phone, literally or metaphorically.

"Ace. Two. Three. Four. Five. Six. Seven . . ." Phillip recited slowly.

"Hello, Mr. Wizard," Spencer said quickly. "Can you tell Trisha her card?"

Phillip heard the noise of the phone being handed over.

"Your card is the seven of spades," Phillip told her with an unidentifiable accent, in a falsetto voice that made him sound like he'd been kicked in the nuts. And then he hung up.

Though his brother had never been farther away, they had fallen back into their familiar—and familial—connection. They didn't know that their mother had learned this trick from her brother, and that by performing it they were communing not just with each other, but with Jenny and Noah and their inescapable shared history of misdirection and wizardry.

Part Eight

Uncle Jerry

Chapter Thirty-One
Brentano's

In the summer of 1959, Jerry Rothstein planned his Fridays so that he could leave work at the jewelry store on 47th Street in Manhattan before four o'clock, allowing him to reach Kellerman's Resort, in Rocky Hill, in the Catskills, before sunset. At his departure hour the parkways were not yet constricted with the thick cholesterol of traffic, and he was able to arrive before the beginning of the Sabbath, when religious Jews were not supposed to drive. Which avoided risking a scene pulling into Kellerman's driveway in his mint-green Cadillac and facing the derision of the very matrons he would need to cultivate to get anywhere near their daughters.

At twenty-three, handsome and husky, with a stentorian voice and a slight accent that lent him a whiff of mystery, Jerry was enjoying a successful summer bedding down girls from throughout the tri-state area. But when he met Jennifer Bernstein he abandoned all previous game plans and shifted his focus.

He first eyed Jenny at the pool. She wore a black bikini with red polka dots, which accelerated the effects of her own geometries. She was curvy and adorable. Instead of the aluminum collar of a sun reflector, she stared down into the pages of a book.

Considering himself a Sherlock Holmes of seduction, Jerry tried to employ cues from a girl's appearance and accoutrements to figure out what might interest her. His wooing was adaptable. With Jenny, he started with the book she was absorbed in, but misread the title, to her genuine amusement, which couldn't be bad. He liked that Jenny seemed unimpressed with him. It intrigued him that a girl from Long Island would deign to rebuff a good-looking successful young jeweler who could regale her with tales of luxury and adventure.

After their brief initial conversation at the pool, Jerry cancelled his evening date with a teacher from Washington Heights. He claimed he needed to meet with a customer who was considering purchase of a large diamond. In fact he was preparing a strategy in response to Jennifer Bernstein having detonated a hand grenade in his heart.

Jenny appeared at the tiki bar that evening with another woman in tow and he steeled himself to impress and entertain Jenny's mother—as he'd charmed the mothers of other girls he'd seduced over the hot Catskill summer. But when they came closer, whispering to each other, he saw that the other woman was young despite a tired quality in her posture. Jerry thought: her sister—the familial tie was obvious in the high, sculpted cheekbones. Something in the sister suggested she was there to protect her sibling. Which was only one of the clues Jerry wrongly interpreted about the Bernstein girls.

He soon recognized the fragile détente between them. What held one's interest sent the eyes of the other roaming the bar or glancing at her wristwatch. He focused the laser of his attention on the younger girl but like the lights from a distant cinema, he also swung them on Phyllis occasionally.

"I am currently reading the new Leon Uris novel. About Israel," Jerry said. He pronounced it "Yis-ra-ail." "Have you read it?"

It was a general question but meant for Jenny.

"Not that one," Jenny said. "But I read *The Angry Hills*. It made me want to visit Greece . . . To see the ruins," Jenny added, but felt she was revealing too much. In her mind Greece was related to Egypt as another ancient civilization with mysterious archaeology inviting exploration. And Egypt was related to Noah.

Jerry noted the tick of excitement in her voice as she talked about books.

"I love any book with Robert Mitchum in it," Phyllis said.

"I thought its literary merits were strong. The book, that is," Jerry said.

"I prefer people over stories," Phyllis added.

Jenny executed a slight eye roll, nearly imperceptible, which she caught Jerry catching. She smiled slightly as if trying to hide it. She nodded, acknowledging that this was exactly right about her sister, passing judgment by simply letting Phyllis speak for herself.

"The best stories are always *about* people," Jerry said.

Jenny liked this burly man despite his over-confidence—and she liked the way he was trying to include both of them in his wooing, though out of politeness or to improve his chances of a successful pursuit she couldn't tell. He was perfect for her sister. Like the double agent in *The Angry Hills*, Jenny launched a counter-mission of her own while thinking about Jack Elliot, whom she would be meeting shortly at the boat dock.

Jerry was one of two sons born to Sephardic Jews who'd barely escaped the holocaust, as they'd escaped threats of the diaspora for hundreds of years. Jerry's father, Abrahan, had been a wealthy diamond merchant in Spain and Morocco and financed the family's own exodus by adroitly doling out finely cut stones (some that were well-cut glass) and small wads of currency sewed into the soles of their shoes. He negotiated their passage like the skillful maneuvering of a taxi driver twisting through the bazaars in Casablanca. The city, not the movie, Abrahan would add whenever he talked about what he always continued to think of as home.

In New York, the Sephardic community embraced the family, as it did so many others who'd made it over. Jerry's father began working in a tiny, dark booth in the diamond district—where, as a teenager, Jerry began his own working career—and progressed to owning his own store in Manhattan and another on Long Island. Jerry and his brother each took over one store—Jerry chose Manhattan because he loved the loud, boisterous, steaming city, how the Chinese and the Irish and the Italians all had their sections, yet crossed paths and intermingled everywhere.

Gold looked good in Jerry's large hands and he was generous to customers who needed his generosity but wily with the rich—mostly gentiles—who came for his expertise. He felt himself a sort of Robin Hood of 47th Street. Even at his young age he donated to charities promoting Zionism and literacy and to the cancer wing of the Jewish hospital. Those who came to know Jerry saw him as a good man if—later on—strict with his wild daughter Leah, who worked *him* like a goldsmith crafting soft metal.

When Jenny left the tiki bar after one drink Jerry determined to win over her sister as a means of getting closer to her. Jenny's coolness was an accelerant to the fire he felt inside him.

Despite himself he fell for Phyllis. He loved the cranky façade she projected, when underneath she was a vulnerable creature who merely wished to be loved unconditionally, to be someone's "the one." Phyllis appreciated the surface nature of his trappings—the mint green car; the thick gold chain with the Jewish letter chai, which meant: life; his familiarity with fine things: diamonds, stereos, the best liquor. She was charmed by how he'd obey the rules of the Sabbath but order lobster in a seaside restaurant on another night, and don the plastic bib without self-consciousness, cracking the bright shells with his strong hands, melted butter daubing his chin.

Still, Jerry's obsession with Jenny never abated. Later that summer, and beyond, he followed the trajectory of Jenny's courtship with Jack Elliot from behind the screen of his own love affair with Phyllis. Their relationship was like a trailing indicator, like a comparative stock chart in which his investment in Phyllis followed slightly behind the trajectory of Jenny and Jack. When Jenny and Jack announced their courthouse marriage only a year and a half after that first weekend at Kellerman's, Jerry waited long enough for his own proposal to seem unrelated. Now that Jenny would marry someone else he deduced that the best way to stay close was to marry her sister.

Chapter Thirty-Two
Archie and Edith

In early September of the summer that the Bernstein sisters met their husbands, Jack Elliot's brother Patrick came up to Kellerman's for a weekend when Jack was able to get some time off. The stream of Manhattan denizens commuting to the Catskills had tapered as kids returned to school and families focused on the fall and winter ahead of them, and the resort was barely half full.

Samuel and Eva allowed the girls to visit on their own that weekend, without parental chaperones. While they were aware that there were now boys involved, they knew resort management would keep an eye on their daughters. They mostly trusted the girls to behave themselves and had lost the energy to enforce restrictions on them anyway.

Jerry Rothstein showed up on Friday evening. When he learned that Jack's brother was joining their usual foursome he saw an opportunity to show kindness and magnanimity to the brothers while also showcasing his own connections.

"I've gotten us tickets to the races on Sunday afternoon," he told the girls on Friday night at the tiki bar. "The owner is a customer of mine and he owed me a favor. Very good seats. In the clubhouse."

"Horse racing, you mean?" Jenny asked. "We've never been."

"No, monkey races," Phyllis said, trying to show how sophisticated she was, although she'd never been to a horse race, either. She was afraid of horses.

"The Catskill Raceway. Harness racing. It's very classy," Jerry said.

Phyllis was pleased. Jenny wrinkled her nose. "Well since Jack's not allowed to recreate on resort property when he's not working, that sounds like fun."

"We'll drink some cocktails, and wear hats," Jerry said.

"We'll pretend we're in *The Great Gatsby*," Jenny said, though neither Phyllis nor Jerry responded to the reference.

On Sunday they drove to the track in Jerry's Cadillac, he and Phyllis in the front, Jenny tucked between Jack and Patrick in the back. For the brothers, it was an escapade, and they loved an escapade. On the drive Jerry explained the rules of pari-mutuel betting, though the Elliot brothers had no plans to gamble their hard-earned capital on a bunch of animals running around in a circle. There would be a band, and they'd all enjoy a few drinks, and watch the beautiful creatures.

At the track the manager ushered them into the clubhouse level. Jerry slipped him a five-dollar bill, making sure they could all see the exchange. Then he sat at the head of their table and focused on the racing form, scribbling in the margins and drawing asterisks next to the horses his analysis suggested might do well.

"He's very good with numbers," Phyllis said.

Jenny was worried that Jack and his brother might be intimidated by the scene, and by the money Jerry was wagering. "You don't have to bet," she told Jack. "We can just pick the winners and see who does better."

"We've been around rich people before," Jack reassured her. "It's okay."

Before the fourth race Jenny reached into her purse. "Would you bet Egyptian Princess for me? Bet her to show; that means third place, right?"

"Yes. Third place," Jerry said, looking at Jack and smiling. "But you will not win very much money."

"So you think this one's a winner?" Jack asked, taking her money.

"I feel very lucky right now," Jenny said, taking his hand.

At O'Rourke's Tavern, in Monticello, after the races, they squeezed into a booth near the bar. The red Naugahyde was split and the table was marked with cigarette burns. A rough crowd of service workers off their shifts shared pitchers of beer in the darker corners, and career drinkers struggled to maintain their purchase on wooden stools at the bar. The jukebox played The Drifters and Ricky Nelson, and that song by Dean DiMucci that Jenny thought of as her own.

Jerry stood out in his Lacoste shirt with the collar up. Jenny and

Phyllis had never been to a dive bar before. Jack and Patrick felt the patrons could have been friends from Rockville Centre or relatives from the old country.

Jack and Patrick ordered Guinnesses, the girls drank Red Devils—vodka and cranberry juice. Jerry had Macallan rocks. The bartender had to climb up to the top shelf of the back bar for the bottle of Macallan. When dinner menus arrived Jack stood on the sawdusted floor amid the peanut shells and hoisted his dark beer.

"Sláinte," he said. "Dinner is on me tonight. Or it's on Egyptian Princess, actually. I won $24 on the horse Jenny picked!" He smiled that devastating smile and Jenny felt the world tilt slightly, like the way globes were offset on their axes.

Jenny understood at that moment that this might be her family—and it pleased her. She felt secure despite the rugged surroundings of the tavern. She imagined this group convening at her parents' house for a holiday—a non-denominational one, like New Year's or the Fourth of July. They would figure it out, they would establish their quirks and mark off the topographies of their individual relationships and come to if not love than at least to respect and be able to rely on each other. Phyllis was a pill but she was Jenny's sister, and would stand up for her if that ever became necessary. Jerry was a show-off but he was strong and loyal. She didn't know Patrick well but she sensed the Elliot boys had been raised well. And Jack, well, Jack was the cornerstone of the vision of the future she was erecting for herself—he'd attend West Point, maybe, and rise through the ranks. She would go to college and write children's books or teach—she was already letting go of the idea of becoming an archaeologist. They'd buy their own home on Long Island, maybe something near the beach, where they could walk with the kids: a boy and a girl, who would be as beautiful and athletic as their father.

Jenny drained her sweet cocktail and stood up the way Jack had earlier. "This is my shout," she said, unsure if that was the right terminology to announce that she was buying the next round. "Here's to Egyptian Princess." She thought about how Noah would have loved this gathering of misfits.

Jack and Patrick grinned at each other. Phyllis and Jerry exchanged glances that suggested they might also smile, as long as it seemed okay with the other one.

Jenny had no way of knowing at that ascendant moment that two of the men at the table would soon be gone from her life, and that she'd have children with both of the ones she didn't love. And that her future would become a series of excursions to foreign places where she could hide in the exotic details of travel rather than confront her sadness—and that she'd pass this same talent at misdirection to the two boys who resulted from her liaisons.

Chapter Thirty-Three

Pes Planus

In 1964—when Jack was long gone and Patrick had moved to Ballydraiocht and the idea of the family Jenny had imagined was demolished, the Bernstein sisters came to Jerry in a rare moment of confluence.

"We have something to ask you," Phyllis said. They were at Phyllis and Jerry's ostentatious house in Woodmere—what Jenny sometimes thought of to herself as "the Garage Mahal," given that most of the street-facing façade was devoted to cars, not people. They were having Shabbat dinner—recipes Jenny recognized from their mother's repertoire.

"I am listening," Jerry said, gnawing on a chicken bone. He was glad that they needed something from him. But seeing them get along made him wary.

Phyllis started it, but faltered. "We were wondering," she said, and then didn't know how to continue. "We were thinking . . ."

"I want another baby," Jenny interrupted. "I don't have a man anymore—and I don't want another one. Would you consider being the father?"

The silence was like waiting for the impact of a comet hurtling toward earth.

Jenny'd already had one child with the brother of her husband, so why not have another with the husband of her sister? There was a twisted synchronicity to it at the same time that it solved a problem.

"You want me to be the father of your child?" Jerry said.

Jenny nodded.

"And you are okay with this?" He looked at his wife.

"We're just talking at this point . . . You've always hoped for a son—a child, at least—and doctors have said that I'm out of the baby business," Phyllis said—although she and Jerry would later prove the doctors wrong when she unexpectedly conceived Leah shortly after Spencer was born. Jenny marveled at how Phyllis had already made this somehow about her own generosity. Possibly she'd done so because she'd always been afraid that Jenny and Jerry might have sex without her approval anyway.

Jerry suppressed the smile threatening to break out of him—trapped inside since meeting Jenny Bernstein in her polka-dotted bikini years earlier.

"This I did not see coming," Jerry said. "But you both know I would do anything for my family."

"We'll all go together," Phyllis said. "We'll wait outside for you."

He shook his head. "We will all go where together?"

"To the doctor's office. You were thinking the casbah?" Phyllis asked sharply, beginning to understand.

Jerry agreed to pose as the child's uncle and mostly stay out of things. Spencer Elliot was born in 1965, fifteen months after Phillip. As he grew, Jenny was glad to see that from most outward appearances the child was her own—irreverent, wild, funny. He'd inherited her fine facial structure and parroted her patterns of speech. But Jenny feared that someone seeing the boy and Jerry together at the pool or the beach might recognize that they had the same feet.

Part Nine

Phillip and Spencer

Chapter Thirty-Four

First Time in a Limo This *Small*

AND THEN THE CALL came from Spencer: Patrick was in the hospital.

"You should probably come now if you're going to," Spencer said.

Phillip was sitting up in the window seat in the attic master suite—"the tower," he and Marty called it—looking west over the lights coming on in downtown Portland. He could pick out the KOIN Tower, the pink U.S. Bancorp building, the white rectangles of the new justice center, and the high radio towers on the West Hills and Council Crest beyond.

"It'll take us a day or two to get there," Phillip conceded. "Any idea how long we should count on staying?"

"If it's up to me I'd have you stay until, maybe, forever?" Spencer said.

"Is anyone saying how long Patrick has?"

"Nobody's saying much of anything, although they do mention the priest a lot. I can't tell if they're joking or they're serious—and I'm not sure there's much difference. I'd guess it could be days, weeks, or months."

"That's very specific."

"It's why they revoked my license to practice medicine."

"Is he cogent?"

"Oh, he's acting as if he'll be back out giving golf lessons next week."

———

Phillip and Marty left for Ireland three days later. At the Portland airport they perused Powell's bookstore and ate street tacos and ducked into the Hollywood Theater's airport outpost to watch a few movie shorts while waiting for the flight to Schiphol and their transfer to Dublin.

They travelled in business class thanks to the last remaining upgrade certificates left to Phillip upon Jenny's death—two years ago now—and Phillip watched *The Princess Bride*. Marty caught him crying at the part where Inigo Montoya says to Humperdinck, "I want my father back, you son of a bitch."

"Did you ever notice how movies on airplanes make people cry much more than the same movies would if they were watching them on the ground?" Phillip asked afterward, wiping at his tear-stained cheeks with a drink napkin.

"I can't say that I have," Marty said.

"Someone should do a study. I've watched films that I would roll my eyes at in exasperation on the ground that had me weeping like a war widow at 35,000 feet. I can't explain it. The airlines should start a 'frequent crier' club and dole out rewards points that you could redeem for logoed hankies."

"You were watching *Elf* again, weren't you?" Marty joked.

If she'd asked about a more imminent crying matter, Phillip couldn't have said how he felt about the fact that his father was dying. He was still processing the discovery of said dad and had in no way incorporated the information—or the father—into his life.

And now, he would have to; or he wouldn't, probably ever. Marty's plan was to make sure that he did, not just for himself, but for the implications this could have on their marriage: Phillip being able to face his emotions head on.

Spencer was waiting for them at the Dublin Airport with a sign that said, "Dr. Galazkiewicz"—a joke from an old Bud Light ad the brothers found hysterical even years after it aired, despite the fact that it wasn't really very funny in first-run.

After hugging they walked out to the parking lot, Phillip and Marty wheeling their Tumi roller bags. Spencer stopped in front of a black Land Rover and opened the back.

"This hit man position is treating you well," Phillip said.

"Oh, the perks are off the charts. If you don't mind the threat of constant murdering," Spencer said. "The Irish are particularly afraid of Jews in the hit man racket. Even the five Jews here who aren't hit men strike fear in their hearts."

Spencer drove them out of the airport and onto the M7. He

handled the car with an almost professional pride, looking the correct way at intersections, cursing at other drivers as any proficient chauffer would, muttering "feck!" only when warranted.

"How are the roundabouts treating you these days?" Phillip asked, a reference to their first driving adventure in Ireland together, when Spencer got caught in one and couldn't find his way out.

"Oh, I've mastered them. Along with escalators and revolving doors. I was top of my class," Spencer said.

"I can't wait until we get to Limerick," Marty said sarcastically, knowing that the brothers' bantering would only accelerate on this long drive as they passed through the unfortunately named town. Unfortunate for her.

"Did I ever tell you about my friend Rod? From Islamabad?" Spencer asked.

———————

They pulled into Ballydraiocht in mid-afternoon and drove straight to Trisha's cottage, where Phillip and Marty would take the upstairs guest suite.

"It's cozy, if a little quirky," Spencer prepared them. "Since there's a pitched roof you pretty much have to walk around on your knees unless you're in the middle of the room. The owls shouldn't bother you unless you make noises like mice in your sleep. And water only comes in when it rains. Which is often, so we've left a couple of ponchos on the edge of the bed."

Trisha shook her head. "It's all bollocks," she said to Marty. "It's a lovely room. Spencer may not feel the same way about where he's staying, though: out in the barn."

They went to the pub for dinner that night and caught up on their diverging lives. It was a new thing for the brothers, who'd never been very far from each other. Nobody mentioned Jenny or quests or unsolved riddles. Nobody talked about who they were in relation to where they were living.

While the brothers free-associated through time and space and referenced Todd Stein from the old neighborhood who'd had a pool table in his garage and built a beaker bong in science class, and they remembered a high school English teacher who used to dress up like Shakespeare once each year, and they discussed the finer points of the pinball machine at the pizza place at the A&P shopping center down the road, and which was the best chocolate bar—the Charleston Chew or the $100,000 Bar—the girls talked amongst themselves. They had much to bond them now, each being married to an Elliot brother, and they commiserated over their plights.

"I'd have had a few things to say to their mother if I'd known her," Trisha commented at one point, shaking a fist in the air.

"She was something, I'll give her that," Marty said. "A force of nature. Like in *Westworld*: her creations got way beyond her control."

"They're a pair, aren't they," Trisha marveled. "I never saw this coming."

"Who could?" Marty said. "It would be like predicting a zombie apocalypse."

"More like guessing that Snooki would get knocked unconscious on *Jersey Shore*," Spencer said, jumping from his own conversation to theirs. "Or that everyone on the Orient Express murdered Johnny Depp. Or that Robert De Niro would appear in *Meet the Fockers*."

"I'll get another round," Trisha said, elbowing her way past Spencer out of the booth. "We're going to need it."

The next morning, after breakfast and strong coffee—Spencer warned Phillip that under no circumstance was he ever to drink a cup of coffee made by Trisha; Spencer described her coffee as "Dunkirk"—they headed to the Elliot house, where Patrick was resting after his most recent stint in the hospital. They'd set up a bed for him in the living room so that when the curtains were open he could enjoy the view out over the Ballydraiocht golf course and the sea beyond.

When he saw Phillip and Marty at the front door with Trisha and Spencer, Patrick insisted on climbing out of the bed. He embraced the newcomers in his weak grasp and tried playing host. He needed help getting to the sofa, but he was dressed nattily in an Under Armour thermal shirt beneath a paisley robe in gold and royal blue. He wore a woolen watch cap with the Ballydraiocht logo. Lorna brought him a cup of tea but after lifting it shakily toward his lips once, he left it to grow cold on the coffee table.

"I'm embarrassed that you had to come all this way just to see an ailing old man," Patrick confessed. "It wasn't necessary. What was it that Lewis Carroll said . . . 'reports of my death have been greatly exaggerated?'"

Spencer refrained from mentioning that the quote was usually attributed to Mark Twain, but that he hadn't actually said it either—but
who cared? Which reminded Spencer of another quote attributed to
Twain that Twain had never said, but it was one of Spencer's favor-
ites, nonetheless: "I have never killed a man, but I have read many
obituaries with great pleasure."

"You look good," Phillip lied to Patrick, just to have something
to say.

"The doctor isn't optimistic. He told me I'll probably need to
hit an extra club from now on," Patrick said. His own optimism—
whether put-on or genuine—was impenetrable. There'd be no talk
of last wishes or tearful good-byes, Phillip realized. Patrick would go
down—as any golf pro would hope for—swinging.

Patrick grew visibly tired from the excitement of seeing some of his
children, new and old—especially the Americans. His energy came
and went like a battery with a loose wire. Several times he nodded
off during the visit, and at one point Lorna said, "Well, off you go
to your luncheon," although they had no luncheon planned.

"Yes, well, enjoy that," Patrick said. "Maybe have a Guinness for
the old man since I've been told to stay off it for a bit. But I would
like you all to come back when the others get here in the afternoon.
We'll have a cup of tea and some cakes. Or you could have an aperitif.
There's something I want to tell you all."

When they came back a few hours later all of Patrick and Lorna's
children had gathered. It was the first time that Phillip met his other
new siblings—Finn, Ciarán, and Conor—and their wives. Peter, the
sibling from Amsterdam, had been back more recently and Spencer
had already begun establishing a relationship with him.

Patrick was sitting behind his desk in the study in crisply creased
blue corduroy pants and a white button-down shirt beneath an argyle sweater. His thinning hair was combed. But he was pale and the
clothes hung off him, the rolled-back sleeves of the sweater revealing
purple bruises on his hands from the IV at the hospital.

Dining room chairs had been arranged around the desk. Phillip and
Spencer sat on a deep couch with their wives, sunk down in the seat
cushions in a way that would prevent them from jumping up even

if the occasion called for it. Trisha was next to Phillip; it comforted him to feel he had an ally in all this. It was an odd alliance in that her husband was still Phillip's brother and best friend. It was confusing even to those of them who were there.

The walls of the study were hung with golf art and photos of Patrick with dignitaries from the sport: Christy O'Conor; Darren Clarke; the golf architects Robert Trent Jones, Sr. and Jr., in separate shots. Jones Jr. and Patrick had met at Ballybunion many years earlier and talked about Herbert Warren Wind and Bach and Imelda Marcos and became fast friends.

"Well, it's not last rites or I'd have called the priest as well," Patrick began. "And he might be here a while to take my final confession when he does come. But there's something I need to confess to the lot of you first."

"Something else besides your ma being English?" Peter asked. He was the sardonic brother who'd probably had his lunch money stolen at school, but was now a powerful corporate executive.

"Oh, this cannot be good," Conor said, before his wife shushed him. Nervous laughter circulated in a weak pulse.

"I'm just going to come out and tell you the upshot and then I'll offer a few words of explanation. And then I'll answer questions if you have any," Patrick said.

"For feck's sake, just get out with it, Da," Trisha said. "If you know who shot JFK, or whatever. Just tell us."

"You've all another brother, is what it is," Patrick said then, and there was an expulsion of laughter—Spencer couldn't tell who it came from—and some gasps and much shaking of heads and looking down at the floor. Ciarán and Conor glanced at each other with wide eyes. They were closest in age and occasionally acted as a single unit.

"Oh, fecking bollocks, you've got to be joking," Padraig said. "Is that all? We were worried it was something serious."

"You were a regular Patrick Appleseed, weren't you, Da," Trisha said.

Johnny Patrickseed would be better, Spencer thought, but did not say this aloud.

"You knew about this one, too, then?" Padraig asked their mom. They all looked over at Lorna.

"Your father had a life before he met me," Lorna said. "This is his business, and it's nothing to do with me."

"So you knew?"

"I knew. Yes."

"I've been true to your mother since they day we met," Patrick interrupted. "And honest about what happened before that. I've not misled anyone. There's no kerfuffle over this between us so please don't manufacture one now. I thought it right to come clean with the rest of you, in case it matters in any way."

"Well, what about this other brother? And please don't tell us his name is Pat," Peter said.

"Michael is his name," Patrick said. "His mother named him. For Michael Collins. And I've no notion what he thinks or what he knows or what he's like or any of that. I've not had any contact with him. I left it to his mother to decide how she wanted to proceed."

"You've been in touch with her, then?" Ciarán asked. He was the other musician in the family. He taught guitar in Valencia and played in a band called The Crackers.

"Not in more than fifty years. I don't know if she's alive or in prison or if she's the Queen of Romania."

Spencer thought: Oh, the Queen of Romania. That's a good one.

"I'll explain it all, if you'll let me," Patrick said tiredly. "Not that there's much to tell . . ." Which was almost certain to prove untrue coming from an Irishman, Phillip thought.

The assembled offspring simultaneously waved at their father with the underhand finger roll an NBA forward might use taking it to the hoop—a gesture they'd either all observed and adapted, or possibly it was wired into their DNA. It was done theatrically, as if to say: "You've stepped in it now, Da, so you might as well get on with it."

Patrick went on to tell them that when he'd landed in Ballydraiocht those many years ago from America he was hurting more from the loss of his brother Jack than even he knew. He was bitter about the Americans' war in Vietnam, how senseless and also solipsistic it was to think you could tell people in another country how they should live, where they could work, what to believe in. It was an affront beyond colonialism.

"Back in Ireland, working at the golf club, I met a young girl at a pub. She'd recently come down from the North, where the troubles were ramping up. It was the same thing there, then," Patrick said. "A colonial power that had taken over a country that wasn't their own, and subjugated the people. That the British still had a hand in running the North was inconceivable. Unacceptable. That Catholics were being oppressed by their own countrymen, supported by the might of a foreign power. I could not abide it. It sharpened the pain and anger I was feeling about Jack's death fighting for America."

The siblings were stunned into silence. Phillip looked around the room at them. *His* siblings.

"Now you're going to tell us that you're Gerry Adams," Peter said.

"No, but I knew him," Patrick said, silencing them all.

Could this be real? Trisha wondered.

And who was Gerry Adams, exactly, Phillip mused, first thinking he'd been a point guard for the Boston Celtics (which he thought of as the *American* Celtics now that he knew about the original ones), before remembering his history.

"I took a leave of absence from the golf club. I told the managers that I had some things to attend to back home in America, that someone was sick. I went North to see the girl."

"I went north," Patrick said again. His eyes looked up with the remembering. He went on to tell them of a three-month period during which he met outlier members of the IRA.

"I believed in a united Ireland. I was a patriot for my own country. It was my newly adopted homeland and I felt even though I'd lived elsewhere my whole life that I had a right to an opinion. Maybe even stronger than if I'd been raised here. The British occupation ate at me. It wasn't until later that I came to understand that it was the pain and the anger from Jack's death that riled me, but back then I wanted to strike out at something. Someone. I wanted to take a stand for my homeland so that it could truly define me.

"The girl introduced me around to her cohorts. They were humorless, violent people—the humorless part being almost as bad as the violence. But they were true believers, and that's what captured me. Their certainty in their cause. It was pure, and beautiful. The girl was all in, and I fell under her spell. The spell cast by all of them, really.

"The meetings were ferocious. You couldn't sleep after a meeting fraught with so much anger and emotion. And whiskey. You went to the pub after. You drank too much. You clung to whoever was around you. We had an affair, me and the girl. It had nothing to do with love or attraction or even comfort, it was an animal thing, we were helpless and bitter for whatever reasons and we threw ourselves at each other. She was a cold one, though—I realized that she'd recruited me.

"As I got further involved their intentions became clearer. They embraced violence in a way that I couldn't. We agreed on many principles, but they didn't care who got hurt. When they started planning what they called 'actions' I knew I'd have to commit at a level I wasn't prepared for. It wasn't in me—hurting people and robbing banks and worse. They called for each of us to decide one way or the other and that this was the time to leave if we weren't up to it.

"So I left. I abandoned the girl, although we'd just learned that she was pregnant. She thought me a coward—not about leaving her and the baby, but because I balked at the violence. I offered to support the child in whatever way I could, to stay in touch. She said it wasn't my child, although I knew it was—we'd been together almost continually for months.

"I hightailed it back to Ballydraiocht—I knew I didn't belong up North—and the club embraced my return here and gave me back my position. I never spoke of this again, ever, to anyone, except your mother. Until now. I'd vowed secrecy, and I felt I owed them that much. Now I'm an old man and this was all a very long time ago and I wanted to get it off my chest to the people I love."

Phillip remained quiet through all of this. He didn't know if he even had a dog in this fight. Since Patrick was only newly his father he wasn't sure he had the right to an opinion on what he should or shouldn't have to tell his kids—the ones he'd acknowledged for their whole lives. He didn't know if Patrick was weak for having acceded to the wishes of the women who'd borne and raised these other children—this woman, and Phillip's own mother, to name two. Phillip didn't know if he was better off for having learned the truth: knowing was always better than not, wasn't it? But getting a father this late just to lose him wasn't the best way this could have gone. So, was it?

Which raised the question of whether they should go off looking for some other poor sod who was in his fifties now—if in fact he was alive—and tell him that his real da was a gentle, dying golf pro in a small town in the Republic, who was formerly an IRA supporter, if only for a few months, but long enough to impregnate his mother before disappearing for half a century. And only a devotee of the cause on a temporary lark that had nothing to do with Irish nationalism but because he'd felt some guilt for his own brother's death in Vietnam and so became a nationalist and fathered a kid who'd more than likely gotten on fine with his life without knowing any of this. Whose own mother had kept this from him for whatever reason, and who the feck were they to go messing with the inner works of a stranger's life when it was already so far along?

And even if contacting him was the right thing, Phillip wondered if he had it in him to go through all this again to find someone who . . . well, he realized . . . who was also his half brother. It was in his nature to get to the rock bottom of every conundrum, but hadn't he mostly let go of the whole Uncle Jumpy mystery? So perhaps there was still a possibility of change for Phillip, too. He wondered: could he let *this* go? Was he meant to?

CHAPTER THIRTY-FIVE
Sharon Curley

SPENCER AND TRISHA AND Phillip and Marty went back to Trisha's cottage. They were off balance from Patrick's revelation and from trying to imagine the gentle old golf pro joining the IRA. Spencer couldn't even make a joke; he just kept opening and closing his eyes as if his vision were blurry and he was trying to reset something to bring the world back into focus.

"I thought we were done with all this," Phillip said to break the silence as they sat at the kitchen table and Trisha made tea. She was allowed to make tea, just not coffee. It was what they did, the Irish—they made tea: to celebrate, to mourn. To discuss.

"All what?" Spencer asked.

"All this intrigue. This ongoing DNA cluster-fuck. Looking for long-lost relatives. Next thing you know a Neanderthal's going to come knocking on the door with a giant mastodon leg, drooling the word for 'brother' and looking for a hug.

"And of all the people to have a secret life," Phillip continued. "I mean one in addition to the secret life he had having fathered me . . . Is there anyone who doesn't have dark secrets, who hasn't spent their life misdirecting those closest to them?"

"I can't really answer either of those questions," Spencer said. "Except to say that I don't have any secrets from you."

They stared out the windows, tracking a light fog rolling landward off the ocean.

"The thing is," Phillip continued, looking down into his cup . . .

"What's the thing?" Spencer asked after a few more moments of quiet—something he could not abide. Still, he employed his "inside" voice. His non-confrontational voice, as Trisha had been trying to teach him.

"I don't even know what the fucking thing is," Phillip said. "Is this even my issue? Is some action required of me? I'm more or less a bystander here."

"It reminds me of a mash up of the best Irish movies," Spencer said. "Like *The Quiet Man* meets *The Commitments* meets *Michael Collins* meets *The Crying Game*. And throw in *Angela's Ashes* and *My Left Foot*." Spencer loved a movie mash up. "It's like John Wayne falls in love with Liam Neeson while they're trying to kill their British oppressors and then returns to his home country and discovers he has a penis. They become politicians while Percy Sledge beats Enya to death in the background and a radical priest delivers last rites and then paints an IRA banner with his feet."

The others were quiet until Marty said, "Maybe more like *Waking Ned Devine* meets *The Snapper*—where an old, naked man riding a motorcycle discovers that his daughter is pregnant but nobody knows who from. Then the old man dies and the town pretends that a lottery winner is the father and then he marries his own brother's sister—oh, wait, that's more like *our* movie . . ."

"Wow," Spencer said, giving them his De Niro face. "I didn't see that coming. Well done."

Trisha brought a plate of chocolate biscuits to the table that nobody felt like eating—although Spencer had three anyway.

"I don't know if it's my issue either," Trisha said, trying to bring them back to the conversation at hand. "I mean, what *is* required of any of us here? Nothing, as far as I can see." Phillip liked the way she said "us."

"But what about the other brother?" Phillip asked. "*Our* other brother? Aren't you curious? Don't we have some responsibility to reach out to him? We have a truth that could be crucial to his understanding of himself. There might be medical info. He may need a golf lesson. And isn't he a part of Patrick's legacy?"

Spencer pointed at his brother as if to say: you go. It was the kind of thing he would have said out loud if he hadn't silently committed to a vow of silence over this current issue that had nothing at all to do with him—a vow that he broke almost immediately.

"You go!" he said anyway.

"Em, nah, I don't think so," Trisha said then. "I disagree. If the lad hasn't come looking for his da, or if his mother who raised him kept it from him, who are we to mess with the whole toboggan?"

"Toboggan?" Spencer said.

"Yeah, I don't know why I said that. It's some kind of sled, isn't it?"

"This is clearly not my toboggan, either. . ." Marty began.

They all gave her the rolling finger thing that meant: carry on.

"Do you all need to agree on this?" she finished.

"Only some of them agreeing is like only some agreeing to a mass suicide," Spencer said. "The ones who don't go along kind of ruin it for the rest."

"Now *that* may be the worst analogy you've ever made," Phillip said.

"Still," Spencer added. "Phillip does love a scavenger hunt, and this is right in his wheelhouse. If he sets out to find the Belfast brother I doubt the whole IRA could stop him."

"I don't think I have it in me," Phillip said then. He sipped his tea, wishing he'd put more honey in it. "I'm out of the reconnaissance business. Even if I decide this is the right thing to do. Which I haven't. This one's not my quest. Maybe I'm still looking for *something*, but I'm pretty sure this isn't it. I'm focused on bigger questions now—even if I don't know exactly what they are."

CHAPTER THIRTY-SIX
David Kaczynski

THE ENSUING WEEK WAS filled with visits to sit with Patrick. He was a beloved figure in Ballydraiocht and environs. One day several of his school classmates came by and the house was filled with tales of drinking and golf, and the coughs of old-man laughter.

Patrick seemed to enjoy the company and the attention at the same time that he wished everyone was making less of a fuss over him. Not even Lorna could tell whether he knew how sick he was and how little time he might have left. Patrick behaved as if his illness was a minor, temporary setback and he'd return to full activities any day. But to his family, especially, it was clear that he was winding down, and they felt sad both for the winding down itself and that Patrick refused to acknowledge it.

Often, the whole array of siblings gathered at the house simultaneously, which gave Phillip and Spencer a chance to get to know the other boys and their families. There was some awkwardness around logistics, as they wondered how long their father might hang on, and whether they'd return home and then come back again for the funeral, or whether something might happen in the next few days. They wanted to remain with Patrick and see this through with him, but what if he lingered for weeks or months?

One afternoon, when Patrick had gone down for a nap, the others retreated to the stone patio out back to get some fresh air. The sun warmed them and they could smell taffy on the breeze tacking in from the ocean. There was an underlying layer of joy in their convocation—Phillip and Spencer could not only feel it, they were included in it. These siblings loved each other, the brothers could see. But they *liked* each other, too.

As they drank tea and coffee and nibbled at scones that Lorna had baked for them, Trisha took it upon herself to address one of the many subjects at hand that they were successfully ignoring.

"I know it's not really the time for this, but what should we do about Michael?" Trisha said to the rest of them. "You know—our terrorist brother?"

They'd begun referring to Michael as "the terrorist brother." They found it darkly amusing.

"I mean, do we call him to tell him about Patrick just to say that by the way, he could come meet his natural father at his funeral?" Trisha went on. "Do we wait till after? Have we decided to just ignore it?"

She glanced at Phillip who was grateful she'd taken this on. He knew she was bringing this up partly on his behalf.

"I've already called him," Peter announced. He was tapping on his phone and looked up to see them all staring at him in alarm. "I found him on the Internet, easy as pie. *Someone* had to contact him," he said defensively.

"Did they now? And it had to be you, didn't it?" Conor said. "Even before any of the rest of us decided on it?"

"I didn't realize it was an issue," Peter said.

"Of course you didn't. Because then you couldn't be the savior, the center of attention."

"Now Conor, lad. I think you're overreacting a little. It's an emotional time for all of us. I was trying to relieve some pressure."

"Were you, then?" Ciarán said.

Phillip and Spencer were beginning to recognize why maybe Peter had moved to Amsterdam and none of the others seemed upset by his absence—at least until he was actually present.

"Well, then, it's done," Trisha said. "No use in arguing over it now."

"Okay, moving on," Padraig said. He was the peacemaker—the middle child who negotiated the hostage crises that the others created. But he couldn't let it go entirely. "So what did he say then? Michael, the terrorist?"

Peter puffed out a laugh. "Actually, he told me he knew all about the poxy golf pro and that I could well fuck off. 'Go fuck a rolling doughnut,' is what he said, which kind of made me like him. I thought: that's my brother!"

"So that's the end of it, then?" Conor asked.

"I imagine so."

"Wait; that's the *end* of it?!" Phillip repeated.

Peter sighed. Now there was a whole new brother to try and make happy. Or at least not make unhappy.

"You have to understand, Phillip. Things are different here," Peter said. He said things as "tings." "You've had only one full brother yourself until recently, but over here siblings are like pints of Guinness. If you miss a round there's always another coming. So while we cherish family, we also have plenty of it. You've just inherited six new siblings—aren't we enough to keep you busy for awhile?"

Which seemed like a fair question.

Chapter Thirty-Seven

Mountain Hardware

PATRICK DECLINED QUICKLY, LIKE a low running drive that finds the speed slot in a fairway and accelerates down hill. In the end he seemed relieved to go, if only because it would take the pressure off everyone else to continue visiting and putting on a happy face.

The morning of his last day he asked to see Phillip alone for a few moments. The windows were all open in the house at Patrick's request—he wanted to smell the grass one more time, and the breath of the sea, to remind him of how fine his life had been. The family bundled themselves in fleece jackets and wool caps. The Irish knew this was the first thing that would be expected of them once their father passed—to open a window to let his spirit free. He'd foreseen this and extended his help even beyond the gentle arc of his life.

Phillip was a mess. He'd been crying out in the kitchen and then grew nervous when the old man called him into the room alone. Marty squeezed his hand.

"I feel like I'm in trouble somehow," Phillip confessed.

"How is that even possible?" Marty asked. "If it was your brother I could understand that. But you?"

"We don't even know each other. What could he possibly have to say to me, separate from all the kids who were his for all those years?"

"That's what you're going find out," Marty said, walking him to the door.

Lorna had propped Patrick up on thick pillows. There was an IV and a full-time nurse. Patrick joked that the IV had run dry of Guinness so now they were giving him antibiotics while the nurse went to fetch another keg.

"I wanted a moment alone with you before the others come in," Patrick said. "Just to tell you . . . what a late game bonus you've been to me these past months. How happy I am that you found me, even for this short while. I know I can't have lived up to the image you had of my brother Jack as your father—the war hero and all—but I just hope I wasn't too much of a disappointment. For me, it's been a lovely gift, totally unexpected. I knew you were out there somewhere all this time and it was a comfort to me. I loved you in a way, if that sounds possible, but I'm blessed to have been able to love you in person, even for this brief time. You've grown into a fine man thanks to your mother. And you'll fall in all right with the rest of them. Just don't let them overwhelm you. I know they're all glad for you, too. They even love your brother, which is a relief because they've been protective of Trisha for a long time. Please keep an eye on Spencer's golf grip for me—I'm leaving you in charge of that. You're the only one who can manage him."

Phillip felt like his mother was dying all over again. He and Patrick were connected through her and he couldn't separate out the pain of missing her from that of losing his father.

"I've also left something for you and Spencer," Patrick said. "I've held it a long time, not even knowing it was meant for you."

Phillip thought back to one of the last things that was left for one of them—to his brother—when Aunt Phyllis had died: the paternity test showing that Uncle Jerry was Spencer's father. And Phillip wondered: is *this* what I've been waiting for?

For Patrick, it all connected back to the brother *he'd* loved so much, whom he'd lost at such an early age. While Phillip never knew Jack himself, it was Phillip's mother and their brief tryst that inextricably tied all these disparate people together in a tight knot that could not be unraveled. These American boys were somehow related to Jack, and carried his spirit forward—even though they weren't really related to him.

"I'm so sorry we didn't have more time together," Phillip said.

"I could have improved your golf game. I could have had you crushing your brother given your natural fluidity. And calm nature. It would have been fun to watch."

"I wish you didn't have to leave us," Phillip said, sobbing into the sleeves of his fleece jacket.

"I'll just think us lucky to have found each other at all," Patrick said. "I'm leaving you in good hands with the lot of them. Now call the others in, would you? I think I'll say a few words to everyone and then I might need to nod off for a while."

Phillip suspected this was Patrick's way of saying he knew it was close to the end. He called the others into the room.

They filed in somberly. The mood was an odd combination of un-fettered sadness cut with wry dark humor. They all loved their father deeply and would miss him every day for the rest of their lives, but they wanted him to go out with amusement and some comfort con-sidering the fine menagerie he'd created, and the legacy—them—he was leaving behind. Finn and his wife Ava brought in their baby, who fussed in his father's arms and then loudly ripped a fart.

They looked around at each other, trying not to laugh.

"Spoken like a true Elliot," Patrick said. "Or perhaps I hear the Pope coming to bless me," he added without cracking his solemn façade.

"But before he does," Patrick went on, "I wanted to say a few words. And this time they truly are few. I've loved you all since the day you landed in my life. I was so happy to be here with every one of you. I loved it here. It was so beautiful—and the more so for getting to watch you all run around in it. I'm sorry to go but I'm excited for what's ahead of me. I suspect that if you continue to behave yourselves I'll see you all there."

Patrick Elliot passed late that afternoon, the sun just gone down and an orange glow above the green hills on the horizon, with only Lorna beside him.

She told them afterwards that he went with a smile, holding her hand. At his request, she'd opened a last can of Guinness for him and poured it into a pint glass. He'd managed one sip, the foam gathering on his upper lip. He'd nodded his head in appreciation.

The old golf pro's last words were pure Patrick, Lorna reported: He'd said, "I'm glad it wasn't a stroke that got me, as I'm sure they would have counted it."

Chapter Thirty-Eight

Black and White Cookies

Neither Phillip nor Spencer had attended an Irish wake before.

"It's not much different than a shiva," Spencer observed toward late afternoon. "Except they don't seem obligated to hide how much they're drinking. And there are no cookies from Walls Bakery."

"The drinking seems to be the whole point," Phillip said.

They looked down into their Waterford glasses of Jameson, admiring the amber color. A parade of well-wishers had marched through the house since early morning bringing food—bowls of stew, casseroles, pasties and cheese platters, and a legion of bottles. Many of the villagers had known about Phillip without ever meeting him and they offered their condolences while sizing him up. They were kind and sympathetic, but also wanted to get a good look at the American who was not just Patrick's son, but the brother of Trisha Elliot's new husband. Oh, and Trisha's half brother, as well.

Phillip overheard two of them talking, mistakenly, about Spencer.

"That's Patrick's son—the new one—innit?" one old codger asked his codger buddy.

"No. That's the other one. The brother. The one that married Trisha."

"Hang on—he married his own sister?"

"No, he married his brother's sister," the second codger explained.

"Oh," the first codger said, nodding as if this made total sense.

The mood in the house—just as at Patrick's last bedside gatherings—was a mélange of "sadness and euphoria," as Spencer described it, misquoting the old Billy Joel song. The brothers were beginning to recognize this as the Irish way—the mood, not the Billy Joel.

As Phillip and Spencer stood by the bar that had been set up in the living room they listened to one of Patrick's oldest mates from secondary school recalling a scene from his own father's funeral to a

194

gathering of other older men. There were a lot of old men, the boys noted. They mostly wore plaid jackets over button-down collared shirts and shoes they looked uncomfortable in.

"When I first came upon Da in the coffin I saw that the corpse had a black eye," the man said. "'Good God,' I said to me brother Liam, 'what have they done to him at the undertakers, he looks terrible.'

"'Oh, that didn't happen at the undertakers . . .' me brother said. ' . . . he wouldn't get into the box!'"

At some point the guests became inebriated enough to overcome their shyness and talk to the brothers. When Phillip mentioned it was his first wake, an elderly gentleman explained the ritual.

"In the olden times we used to drink our stout from pewter mugs, and some people consumed enough of the delicious liquid to get lead poisoning. One of the effects was a catatonic state. So when an old drinker died his mates would stand guard around the body for a few days before burial . . . in case he was to wake up."

"You're joking," Spencer said. He looked down at his own glass which he was happy to see was made of, well, glass.

"God'll strike me if I am," the man said, clinking glasses with Spencer. "Sláinte, young man."

In the late afternoon there was a lull in visitors and Phillip and Spencer thought the wake was winding down.

"Ah, no," Trisha said. "I'm afraid not. There'll be pipes at some point and then his closest friends will arrive for the night vigil . . ."

By pipes she meant bagpipes, which sounded as darkness gathered, first far off in the distance like the low moaning of someone with a stomach flu, and then louder as the piper walked the road to the house and it sounded like someone was strangling a sheep. Behind him came a cadre from the golf course who were looking forward to their last night with Patrick on this earth. Irish tradition held that the body could not be left alone between death and burial, and close friends came to give respite to the family so they could get some sleep. In truth, the Irish were drawn to a party that would run all night, where they could tell their stories with no hard stop.

By midnight the house was full mostly of men who tried admirably to smoke as much as they drank—stepping outside for cigarettes and pipes, some of the younger men vaping fruity white clouds. The brothers took the opportunity to light up Arturo Fuente Hemingway

Classic Dominican cigars on the back patio. The air was bracing and smelled of fried fish and meat pies.

"Well, that's the end of it," Phillip said as they puffed into the clear night.

"The end of it?" Spencer said.

"The last of our parents," Phillip said. "Which means we're next."

"That's a cheery thought the night before a funeral," Spencer said.

"A mere observation," Phillip said. "That there's no generation now between us and the inevitable end."

"Have you considered stand-up comedy?" Spencer asked.

Phillip took a deep draw off his stogie, tilted his head up, and sent a cloud of smoke into the star-sprinkled black sky. He ruminated again on the Native American tradition in which every exhaled puff was a prayer sent upward toward the Great Spirit. His own prayer this time was for clarity, and to make his remaining years as productive and hilarious as possible. Which meant he needed some direction on where to spend those final years. He'd thought there was plenty of time to write a new chapter for him and Marty out west. Now he wasn't as certain. Was it too late to be waiting for a new hand? Should he be happy to play the one already dealt to him, although the cards were slightly bent from so much shuffling and the ten of diamonds had a crimp in one corner? Should he stop mixing his metaphors?

"And there's nobody coming up behind us, either," Phillip said. He flicked ash on the stones of the patio. "Are you ever sorry that you didn't have kids?"

"I hate kids. I've always hated them. I hated myself when I was a kid. They're loud. And sticky. And they constantly need money for toys and clothes and food, but they never contribute. They can't even work for the first two or three years, from what I'm told."

"So what's your legacy? What are you going to leave behind you so that people will remember you?"

"If I'm lucky, you'll be my legacy. You'll write the saga of Spencer. It'll be like Keats's poem. But your Spencer tribute will be *Ode on a Grecian Formula*."

"Nobody will remember me, either," Phillip said. "I may leave some money to my college, but that's about it."

"So, like a Mallomars behest? Or an annuity that buys a pair of boating shoes for every freshman?"

"Chips Ahoys would be more likely, but I was thinking I might fund a literary prize, actually," Phillip said. "But I can't help thinking it was selfish of us not to cultivate another generation of little Phillips and Spencers . . ."

"Hang on a second," Spencer said, tapping his cigar on the patio wall so that the ash dropped off, leaving the end of it a round glow like the fire ringing an eclipse of the sun. "You think it was selfish *not* to have children? So you feel that there aren't *enough* humans on the planet and we should have done our part to add a few more resource-guzzling rich white folk? You're the environmentalist in the family and you're advocating for *less* population control?"

"I'm thinking about what we've accomplished here."

At that moment two adolescents burst out the back door. Spencer could swear the second was carrying a half full bottle of whiskey beneath his coat. They had skateboards under their arms and attempted skating down the grass lawn and ended up in a laughing heap.

"We both found people to love, and that's not nothing," Spencer said.

"There is that," Phillip said. "Now we just need to find our place in the world."

"*Isn't* that our place? Who could have imagined both of us ending up married in the later innings, just when we were ready to stand and stretch and sing *Sweet Caroline* by ourselves. And now there's someone else to buy a hot dog for."

"Yes, but we'd better eat it fast," Phillip said.

"This death business has turned you morbid," Spencer said. "There's almost nothing amusing about it. It's got to stop."

"It'll all stop," Phillip added, and they looked at each other and touched their cigars together in a weird, Elliot sort of toast.

Chapter Thirty-Nine
Me Transmitte Sursum, Caledoni

THEY BURIED PATRICK ON a fine summer day that would have been perfect for golf. A peat fire was burning in a field nearby and the air tasted like whiskey and cigars.

The family gathered at Lorna's house and then made their way to the church—Patrick would be buried out back in the old graveyard with listing stones from as early as the seventeenth century, beside his parents, who'd chosen to be buried in their homeland rather than in their adopted country. He wouldn't be joining any of his siblings, as those who'd passed had been buried in the States. Except for Jack, whose remains probably lay in the Vietnam jungle despite the military insisting he'd been found and shipped home. A large oak cast shade on the stone church and birds could be heard stuttering in the branches.

At the gravesite, following the Latin mumblings of the priest, Patrick's friends and family and neighbors filed past the hole and threw handfuls of dirt onto the coffin, many wishing him a personal goodbye. They crossed themselves and closed their eyes as if imagining that the gentle old man they'd loved and admired and aspired to be like was still there with them.

When the majority of the crowd had begun making their way to their cars to drive to the pub for one last pint in the golf pro's honor, Phillip and Spencer stayed behind in the cemetery. Trisha and Marty hung back with them. The women exchanged glances, each hoping the other knew what the boys were up to—and could stop it if necessary.

Several shovels stood in the pile of dirt beside the grave and Phillip and Spencer each took one and continued to fill the hole.

Padraig came chuffing back to the Elliot plot when he spotted them. "Oh there's no need to do that," he said in alarm. "There's gravediggers for that, you know. They'll get it sorted."

"We'd like to do it," Spencer said.

"It's an old ritual in our tradition. In the Jewish tradition," Phillip said. "I hope you won't mind. The Talmud says that burying someone you care about is the final proof of your love for them. Because it's the one kindness you perform knowing that it can never be repaid."

"Ah, that's lovely," Padraig said. Then he returned to the cars and gathered up his other siblings and brought them back to all help send Patrick off.

When the family arrived at St. Urant's Pub, the mourners were rating the priest's sermon. Phillip could hear some of their criticisms from the bar.

"It wasn't his best work. Barely a literary reference and not a single golf term," an old farmer said.

"He wasn't on his game, that much is certain," another added. "Not even the old saw about God not being able to hit a one-iron, which he drags up whenever a club member dies."

"I don't know, Danny," another said. "You can't hold him to the standards he set as a younger man. He's seventy years old. I loved what he said about the offspring."

"That was some fine work, I have to go along with Bobby," said one of them . . ." I appreciated the dryness of his humor . . . and that line about Patrick and Rory."

"There was a bit much Latin for my own taste," another added, and the others nodded their heads at something they could all agree upon.

At the end of the day Phillip and Trisha stood out on the back patio of her cottage. Spencer and Marty were in the kitchen putting together food.

"Well, I couldn't have seen this coming," Phillip said looking off into the dark night.

"Which part is that?" Trisha asked.

Phillip looked at her face and recognized aspects of his own in it—which was still unnerving. "Standing out here with my sister. Who's my brother's wife. Mourning the passing of my father fifty years after he was supposed to have died—even though it's a different father. An actual one. Mourning him in Ireland. My partial homeland. None of those things would have been imaginable even two years ago."

"It's a lot to absorb. Perhaps you'd like to stay a little longer to get it all sorted?" She said this quietly, as if she could slip it past him unnoticed.

Phillip didn't answer and she said, "Your family is here. Not just Spencer, but all the rest of us. We're what you've got left with your mom and your aunt gone, and only cousin Leah, but you don't see much of her anyway. You could call it home, at least for a while."

"I never considered it," Phillip said. He wondered if *this* was what Jenny had pointed him toward. "It makes a kind of sense when you look at it that way."

"You've had a series of shocks these past couple of years, and your mother's death was the least of it. Everything you knew was pulled out from under you."

"Spencer would offer a movie mash-up right about now to describe it all."

"He would for certain," Trisha said. "My husband, Spencer."

She said it with such tenderness that Phillip was moved. They'd discovered love so late and so unexpectedly that it reminded him of his own luck in having a reboot with Marty. He and Marty very well *could* live in Ireland. But the more he dwelled on it, picturing the mountains outside Portland and the new real estate project, the wineries and coastal views, his image of throwing a ball to a handsome dog on a sprawling lawn behind a stone mansion—even though he'd never had a dog or a lawn or a stone mansion—the more he realized: he'd always expected that he and Spencer would both return to New York.

Chapter Forty
Fortiter Et Recte

The day after Patrick's funeral, Lorna drove over to Trisha's cottage. Spencer was making French toast and delivering a diatribe on whether it should really be attributed to the French. Then he got going on Belgian waffles. And why Europe had a claim on all the best breakfast foods.

"And what's up with grapefruit?" he went on. "It has nothing to do with grapes. We don't say 'orange fruit.' We don't say 'steak meat' or 'tomato vegetable'—although a tomato is actually a fruit—so we don't say 'tomato fruit.' We do say 'jack fruit' but that's to distinguish it from *people* named Jack, which makes total sense."

"I have something for the boys," Lorna announced when Spencer paused long enough for someone else to speak. She sat down in the kitchen. She saw the coffee pot on the counter but opted for tea just in case Trisha had made the coffee. "I'd like to give it to them privately."

The brothers looked at each other. They'd been waiting a long time for something.

In the study at the back of the house Lorna took an envelope out of her bag and handed it to Phillip. "Patrick wanted you both to have this," she said.

Phillip's first thought was: something from Jenny—that she and Patrick had been in touch over the years, after all. Spencer was in a roil and couldn't think of what might be coming down the pike.

"It's a letter. From Jack," Lorna said. "Patrick's brother. The man you thought was your father all those years. Patrick was quite sure it was meant for the both of you."

Phillip slid the letter out of the envelope. He thought of the Uncle Jumpy letter he'd abandoned in Portland. Attached to the top, with yellowing tape, was a small silver ring with a blue stone etched with gold veins. The letter read:

Dear Patrick:

I wish I could tell you where and how I am but I've little idea of either and cannot communicate any real info at any rate as it will be redacted and I fear this letter might not reach you.

I am enclosing a ring that Jenny sent to me for good luck. It has worked well to this point, but I am fearful that its powers may soon run out—they are being tested more each day. The ring was from her beloved brother Noah, who died suddenly. The stone is lapis lazuli, which was sacred to the ancient Egyptians, whom Jenny revered. She never talks about her brother but I know the ring was precious to her. Which is why I enclose it here. I would not want the ring lost to her and as I don't know where I am headed, I entrust it to you to return it if something should happen to me. Otherwise I will reclaim it from you, and Jenny need never know.

I'm sorry not to have been a better correspondent these past months but it has been harrowing here in the jungle— which is already more than I should say.

I wish you the best at the Lawrence Club—I expect you'll be the Head Golf Professional by the time I return, and you'll have to give me even more strokes in our next match.

Love to Mother and Father and the others, and yes, even to you, my brother.

Jack

The original address on the envelope was Patrick's and Jack's parents' house in Rockville Centre, but it had been forwarded to Ballydraiocht—implying Jack did not even know that his brother had moved overseas. Sometimes letters to and from Vietnam took months to get through the censors and reach their intended recipients.

Sometimes a letter only arrived at the right place after nearly half a century.

"Patrick said that he meant to give the letter to your mom when he saw her again, but that never happened," Lorna said. "Then he meant to send it to her, but life got in the way—both hers and his own."

Phillip separated the ring from the page—the ring that Noah had bought, coincidentally, from Jerry Rothstein, when Jerry worked at his father's tiny booth on 47th Street, long before Jerry entered their lives; the ring Noah gifted to his sister from beyond the grave, who sent it to Jack Elliot in Vietnam to protect him, which it did for a while, before he sent it for safe keeping to his brother, who held onto it for decades in Ireland because it soon reminded him of his own dead brother and he never found the right opportunity to return it, before passing it to Phillip and Spencer—closing a loop they would never recognize, connecting them all through time and space and memory in ways they would never know, and completing a quest that their mother was unaware that she'd sent them on. Not a quest to solve, so much as a quest to live: to go forward together as family.

Epilogue
Szechenyi

"I HAVE AN IDEA," Phillip said later that day when the four of them sat in the living room sipping Irish whiskey and watching light drain from the sky.

"That's almost never good," Spencer said. "The last time you had an idea the Mets traded Nolan Ryan and 200 other players to the Angels for Jim Fregosi."

"What's your idea, sweetie?" Marty said. "It's not another invention like when you thought up the edible massage table head rest?"

"We should go traveling," Phillip said. "All of us together. To Europe, maybe."

"We're already in Europe, Magellan," Spencer said.

"The part that's on dry land. That's not an island," Phillip countered. "Italy. Spain. Turkey. Mainland Europe."

"Turkey's technically partly in Asia," Trisha pointed out.

"Have you all secretly become cartographers?" Phillip asked. "Would you like to tell me how the Bosphorus divides the former Constantinople so that half is in Asia and half is in Europe, and then tell me about the Chain Bridge and what happened at Gallipoli?"

Spencer seemed to consider this. "The Chain Bridge is in Budapest, but that's beside the point . . . And we should suddenly go traveling together because why?" he asked. "Don't you still have fence line to run or trains to rob out in the Oregon Territories?"

"For one thing, it would honor Mom. Traveling was her true love in life. After Jack died, anyway. Maybe that's her legacy to us. And to honor Jack, too, and the life he never lived. And because we're rich and underemployed and have new wives to show off to. And because we can. And because it might be good for us. And might reveal things to us. Maybe even wonderful things. If that's enough reasons."

204

"I like it," Spencer said.

"I've some additional time off to burn," Trisha added. "I like it, too."

"What about Egypt?" Spencer said then. "Mom loved everything Egyptian."

"I've always wanted to see the pyramids," Marty said. "But I'm not riding on a camel, I want to make that much clear in advance."

"Duly noted: No camel rides. I've always wondered why the Egyptians didn't build any other shapes than pyramids," Spencer said. "I mean, what's so special about them? What about cubes and even circles, or I guess spheres would be the comparable round three-dimensional shape, which have worked pretty well for buildings for some time now? What about rhombuses, even though I don't know what a rhombus is?"

"Is there a way to make him stop?" Trisha asked.

"None that we've discovered," Phillip said.

"Do you fancy hitting him on the head with a hurling stick would have an impact?"

"Only on the hurling stick."

Spencer smiled as if to say "thanks." "Turning back to the travel notion," he said. "When could we go?"

"I might need some time to figure a few things out first," Phillip said.

"You mean like the Fibonacci sequence? Or where you left your wallet?" Spencer asked.

"Marty and I need to deal with Portland."

"It's another fine mess you got us into there," she said only slightly misquoting Oliver Hardy, although she did not poke Phillip in the eye or smack him with a shovel.

"I'm not sure what I was thinking," Phillip said

"You were thinking you were Johnny Cash or Hank Williams or Dwight Yoakam. You killed a man named Mr. Jones in Reno just to watch him listening to hillbilly music and setting the woods on fire while deciding whether to ride a pale horse on a lonesome highway or a pony on a boat . . ."

"I truly don't know how you do it," Trisha said.

"I can't help myself," Spencer said.

"It's a funny thing about travel," Phillip said. "When I'm home I dream about exotic locations. But when I'm away I pine for the simple comforts of home—like drinking my morning coffee overlooking the trees and the brownstones and the dog walkers, or jogging The Ramble in Central Park, or getting a pepperoni slice at Famiglia's.

"So when you say 'home' you seem to mean New York," Spencer observed.

"That hasn't gone unnoticed," Phillip said and he glanced at Marty; she gave him that look that said she was right about something that he'd disagreed with and now she'd been proven right and he should be sheepish and conciliatory—which were both unlikely.

Looking out at distant golf flags snapping in the wind, Phillip thought about them all traveling together, and pictured them in a boat on the Nile, toasting Jenny. And Jack. And while they were at it, the rest of them, known and unknown: their ancestors.

The next day, when they were heading to the pub for a fish and chips dinner on Phillip and Marty's last night in Ballydraiocht, Phillip said—apropos of nothing—"Travel is where you go to discover your true home."

They looked at him, trying to place the adage. They realized it wasn't an adage, that it was a Phillip-age. And that it was Jenny's final gift to them.

"That sounds like an epigraph for a novel," Spencer said. "Like it comes before a poignant story about the best brother who ever lived, probably with a name like Spencer."

"A book like that would likely have a tragic ending," Phillip said.

"If I was a novelist I'd write a book called *Everyone Dies*," Spencer said, "and then in a twist at the end, nobody would die. Or maybe only one person. Probably the hero. But not a hero named Spencer. Spencer would live on to fight another day. He'd become king of the cowboys. And I would end the book with the word . . . 'nah.'"

"I know what's coming," Phillip said.

"What's that?" Spencer grinned because he knew his brother knew.

"Discussion of who's going to play you in the movie."

"Antonio Banderas. Or Enrique Iglesias. Or another gorgeous but undiscovered Spaniard of a certain age. But definitely not Javier Bardem, because he looked too creepy in *No Country for Old Men*. His haircut made him look like Moe from *The Three Stooges*."

So they would go to Egypt.

A plan had been made to make a plan. It was as much as they were capable of at that point. Two brothers who loved each other, traveling together, with their wives, to a place beloved by the only parent they'd known. Something their parents never got to do. That Jack and Patrick Elliot never got to do. The boys' legacies were each other, and the odd families they'd built; if there was an answer to their quest it was each other.

Trisha and Spencer drove Phillip and Marty to the airport in Dublin for their flight back to Portland via Amsterdam. Spencer unloaded their baggage from the Land Rover. They stood at the curb at the airport knowing that security would eventually decide they'd been there long enough saying goodbye and urge them to get moving. They hugged in all the various permutations.

"Eventually we'll have to figure out what's next," Spencer said. "Not just our spring break romp in Egypt, but with other minor stuff—like where we're all going to live."

And they looked at him, and in unison, as if they were family— which they were—the others shook their heads and said, simultaneously, ". . . nah . . ."

Acknowledgements

THANKS—AGAIN—TO DEDICATED and tireless early readers James Latham, Kieran Devine, Reneé Renfrow, and Brad Studstrup. Also to Dan Pope, the best book doctor a recovering novelist could be lucky enough to encounter. And on going thanks to the members of my monthly writers' group: Tim O'Leary, Maureen Sullivan, David Frost, Darrel Williams, Kim Croft Miller, and Marti Mattia.

Many friends and colleagues have been graciously kind and generous in supporting my fiction, sharing my posts, providing encouragement, expressing (or at worst feigning) great excitement, and otherwise helping to make a small-press, literary novel a success—no easy feat in the current publishing climate. Special thanks in that regard to Karen Moraghan at Hunter Public Relations, who is always relentless in her support and efforts just because she can be. And nobody has worked harder on my behalf than Kelly Huddleston and David Ross at Open Books.

To anyone else who reads these sorts of things, don't forget to buy small-press books, buy from publishers and local bookstores, and do what you can to keep your writer friends from a life of crime. Do it for the children.

Made in the USA
Middletown, DE
01 March 2022

61908756R00130